The Golden Salamander

The Fire of Hell.

Ernest J Swain

Prologue

'The Golden Salamander' is a story of extremism, jihad, and an attack on the city's airport that results in bloodshed. The story develops into a hostage situation in which Angie, the wife of Mike Borman, our main character, is involved.

Just imagine for a moment how you'd feel if your wife was in danger and you were in a position to help her and yet you were being obstructed by someone obsessed by the dictates of regulations and 'red tape'. Feelings run high and actions are not always rational in such circumstances. Unbelievable? Not at all, read on.

Chapter 1

The presentation.

Mike was fed-up to the back teeth and he tried to briefly hide from the melodrama leaving Angie, his wife, sitting proudly on the front row of the semi-circle of seats in the Assembly Room, chatting enthusiastically with her friends. They were all full of pride in ©their husbands, eager to share in the reflected glory of the event. It was an undoubted step up on the social ladder.

Angie's blonde hair had taken an age that morning at the salon and the coiffeur had certainly excelled himself. Her tall slender figure in navy two-piece over the frilly blouse and matching high stiletto heeled shoes, had all created an effect that always brought such admiring glances from men, and she knew it. She certainly knew how to attract attention and she played it for all it was worth.

Mike, on the other hand, found this circus a pain in the backside and he stepped outside into the corridor to escape the chit-chat and what he saw as false bonhomie that always surrounded these presentations. The sooner it was over, the better, as far as he was concerned. Little did he know that this was a prelude to what would become a life- threatening episode in the near future. Even out in the corridor he couldn't escape,

"Borman, Why aren't you in best uniform?" asked the three-pip general (as Mike always dubbed the uniform Chief Inspectors – especially those full of their own importance). Mike looked at him with undisguised contempt, but he made no reply. His thoughts at that moment were quite derogatory and were better kept to himself.

To his mind they were mostly empire builders who had never done a practical day's policing in their careers. Some of these 'fast-tracked' upstarts that came out of the universities, full of academic qualifications but with little or no common sense were an embarrassment. They'd probably never been exposed to any form of danger in their lives and yet guaranteed promotion out-stripping those on the business end of the job. It really got up Mike's nose.

Obviously the Chief Inspector thought better than pursue the question, reading Mike's mind quite accurately, and instead entered the Assembly Room to orchestrate the presentation.

As the Chief Constable entered in all his regalia and splendour, accompanied by the Chairman of the City's Police Authority, Councillor Goulder, Mike took his seat alongside Angie. although his heart wasn't really in the occasion.

He looked at Angie with pride, she had the eye-catching looks that could have opened many doors; to a career in modelling perhaps.

The other seats alongside the Chief Constable, facing the semi-circle, were taken up by the Chief Inspector, Detective Superintendent Alan Birchall (Mike's own governor) and Councillor Goulder, chair of the Police Authority of the Crenarth City Council.

The Chief Inspector stood to the lectern and slightly adjusting the microphone, he tapped lightly with his finger to bring the gathering to attention, and then with his note-pad before him, he began;

"Ladies and Gentlemen and members of the press, it's my pleasure to open this presentation with a brief resume of the events leading up to today. We're here to present certificates of our Chief Constable's commendation for bravery to three officers. Those three officers have already been commended for their outstanding bravery by Her Majesty's Judge of Assize, Mr. Justice Blaze, who described the enquiry as "...one of endurance and tenacity that resulted in acts of astounding bravery.

"These three officers....." and he paused to give a sweep of his hand to indicate Mike and his two companions, "..... undertook a most difficult covert operation that involved some extremely nasty individuals, all with extensive police records for violent crime. The enquires involved other countries of Eastern Europe." He paused to give dramatic effect, then continued,

"At the culmination of that enquiry these officers were faced with a group of five men who were armed – and willing to use their weapons. Never-the-less, they were overpowered and disarmed, and they have all received long terms of imprisonment."

The Chief Inspector then lifted his gaze to the rear of the gathering, addressing the members of the press and photographers, he said,

"For the benefit of the press, we have produced a sheet of facts, identifying the officers, with full details of the five offenders, and the charges against them, which include Attempted Murder, Grievous Bodily Harm, Trafficking for Prostitution, Procurement, serious sexual offences and possession of Firearms. A transcript of the sentences handed down by Mr. Justice Blaze and his commendations for the officers' bravery, is also shown."

Mike was preoccupied with the Councillor who seemed to be paying rather a lot of attention towards Angie. Almost every time Mike looked towards him his eyes were fixed on Angie. A jealous feeling began to burn inside.

Returning to address the whole gathering, the Chief Inspector then said,

"It is my pleasure to introduce Sir Charles Cornell, the Chief Constable of the City of Crenarth Constabulary".

Sir Charles approached the lectern nodding his appreciation to the Chief Inspector and began,

"Words are quite inadequate to express my admiration for these three officers. In all my years in the Police Service, I have never cease to be amazed at the zeal, the fortitude and the raw bravery that my officers continue to show in upholding the law and bringing offenders to face justice." The Chief constable adjusted his reading glasses before continuing,

"Apart from their outstanding bravery in arresting five armed aggressors, these three officers showed exceptional ability in a complex enquiry and showed steadfast determination in the face of hostile cross examination at Crown Court. I concur with the remarks of Mr. Justice Blaze, at Crenarth Crown Court, 28th June, 2007, when he commended these officers for their bravery. I shall proudly enter the commendations upon their service records.

I now turn to Councillor Herbert Goulder, the Chairman of the City Police Authority, and ask him to present the certificates and citations.

"First Detective David Scott," announced the Chief Inspector.

As David stepped up to the rostrum the Chief Constable was first to shake his hand to the applause of the select little crowd. Shaking hands with Councillor Goulder he accepted his framed citation and stood, maintaining the handshake, for the benefit of the cameras.

"Next Detective Parr", and Andrew stepped up for the handshakes and the photographs.

"What a bloody charade", Mike whispered to Angie.

"Finally, Detective Sergeant Borman."

With reluctance Mike got to his feet and stepped forward. He respectfully shook the hand of the Chief Constable and moved across to face Councillor Goulder. His piercing gaze fixed Goulder, and for just seconds, time seemed to stand still. Nothing was said but the hesitation and the stare was quite unsettling for Goulder. He held out his hand to Mike but the response was the merest of touches, and having accepted his framed citation, Mike backed away, deliberately keeping his face turned from the flashing cameras. Everyone must have noticed the atmosphere that existed between the two men, in fact there were several nudges amongst the audience.

"What more can you expect from him?" came a purposely audible remark from some female close behind Angie, who inwardly recoiled at the put-down.

Mike made his exit from the room holding the citation aloft against his face to prevent photographs and he was part way down the corridor when Superintendent Birchall ran after him.

"Mike. Mike. What the devil's got into you?"

"Oh, I'm just sick of this publicity merry-go-round."

"Damn it Mike, even the Chief noticed. We'd better have a talk. Come to my office, we'll have a brew."

"Look Guv, I've got to see my wife off, give me twenty minutes and I'll be back."

Outside in the car park Angie showed her anger and disappointment,

"Mike Borman, I shall never forgive you. You've got to spoil every damned thing for me haven't you."

"Angie, I don't expect you to understand. I live with this every blasted day of my life."

"Understand ? What's there to understand? Just your pig headed arrogance......." and she let her sentence fall away, unfinished. Mike held open the door of her car whilst she climbed inside.

"I'll see you later. I'm not sure what time I'll be back. I've something to attend to", he said as he firmly closed the door, and blew her a kiss.

"Yes, and up yours too. Dinner will be at seven and if you're not there – hard luck," she said under her breath as she drove away.

Chapter 2

Paranoia

Back at Birchall's office, Mike knocked and walked in without invite.

"Now Guv, you were about to tear me a strip off."

He took a chair, reversed it, and sat astride with his arms folded over the back-rest.

"Take a seat. Why don't you?" Birchall said with a degree of sarcasm, "You know Mike, you've got the most appalling manners, and one day they're going to cause you some grief. You've clearly no respect for rank at all."

"You know me Guv and you've got my total respect. I give it where it's due. It's a double edged sword. If I get respect, I'll give it in return".

Alan Birchall was a lot closer to Mike than most others in this hierarchy and despite Mike's irreverence toward rank, Birchall considered him a real asset. On the other hand Mike considered the Chief Superintendent a friend, and despite his almost intolerable disregard of respect for rank, he still felt a deference to Birchall. Calling him "Guv" would have been unforgiveable to another officer of that rank but Birchall, a Londoner, was accorded this address simply because it was commonplace in the Metropolitan Police and he readily accepted it from his own detectives.

"Look here Mike, I'm sure you know, you're making enemies – especially the uniform branch, and there are murmurings already. They'll get you Mike if they make up their minds to do it. I've seen it before. They'll watch you like a hawk and they'll examine every last little detail especially your expenses claims, and the very slightest thing they find wrong, they'll drop on you like a ton of bricks".

"Murmurings? What do you mean? Who?"

"Look Mike, I can't say too much but the word is out about your total disrespect for superiors."

"Superiors? I don't regard any of the bastards 'superior' to me. They're higher in rank than me but they're in no way superior."

7

"Good God man, you're showing signs of paranoia", said Birchall as he poured the boiling water onto the tea bag. He was prepared to give Mike a good deal of latitude but felt he had to be reigned in a little.

"It's not paranoia Guv, its bloody frustration and anger at the way they treat people."

Mike watched as his boss poured the milk into the two mugs,

"It's milk, no sugar isn't it?" Mike just nodded and then said,

"It's this last business that's really got my goat. The judge acknowledged the bloody danger we faced and then you, yourself, recommended the three of us be considered by the Home Secretary for the Queen's Police Medal but some faceless little bastard up there in the Kremlin decides that the degree of bravery we'd shown wasn't sufficient. Some bloody stuffed-shirt pen-pusher, who's never been exposed to danger in his whole life. I just wish I could meet the little turd. Then, after all this, they

have the bloody audacity to ask the three of us to take part in a force publicity stunt, wanting to publish our photographs and give full details of our life, our families and even our homes – just the sort of information that these bastards we've 'banged up' want, so that they can take their revenge at some stage."

Mike threw his hands in the air to show his frustration,

"For God's sake, we're supposed to be Special Branch, an organisation that prides itself in secrecy and covert operations, and then our own people want to publish our bloody photographs and expose us to the world. There doesn't seem any sense up there in the politburo. Then you call me paranoid? I'm sorry Guv, but if that's paranoia I suppose I'll have to hold my hands up."

The two sat in silence for a brief moment whilst they sipped their tea. After a while Birchall spoke again,

"Well Mike, you're right I suppose, it was insensitive…" and before he could continue Mike interjected,

"Insensitive? Insensitive? It was a bloody sight more than insensitive, it was bloody criminal ineptitude, almost asking that someone take a pot shot at either us or our family."

Birchall continued,

"You're right. I can't argue with you about it, but what I'm trying to get over to you is that you've got to let it go. Forget it. Because if you don't you're going to bring grief on yourself. They're going to get you – one way or another – and I don't want to see that happen."

"O.K. Guv..." Mike answered, "...I appreciate what you're saying and I'll watch my back."

Birchall held out both hands, palms facing Mike in a gesture of exasperation and said,

"Well, all that apart, what gives with the councillor, Herbert Goulder. What's he done to you?"

Mike placed his empty mug down on the tray and then said,

"It's personal Guv. I'd rather not say too much."

Birchall raised his eyebrows and said,

"Well, I can't make you tell me if you don't want to, but whatever it is, just remember who you're dealing with. He's got a lot of clout in this job and the 'brass' are going to lean heavily to his side unless you've got some very sound reason to treat him like that – especially in public."

"OK Guv, I'll tell you. The bastard was leering at Angie, and I wanted to let him see how I felt about it. I appreciate what you're saying but I won't put up with that."

Mike's blood pressure seemed to be at boiling point as he left the Superintendent's office, feeling so frustrated and angry, and thinking 'what else would anyone expect of me, with a lecherous bastard leering at my wife. Would they be so eager to defend him if it was their wife?'

The drive out to the suburbs to his smart little semi was a chance to calm down and for once in his life he concentrated on his driving, keeping within the limits and stopping at each set of lights immediately they showed amber – not his usual practice. If the uniform branch were intent on some sort of retribution he didn't want to give them an easy opportunity.

His inner turmoil had led him away from his usual route home, to this salubrious leafy avenue where he now parked. It was obviously an estate agent's dream location where each house was detached and had beautifully manicured gardens, nothing like his own three up and three down. He switched off the engine and sat there in silence looking up the gravelled driveway to this large mock-Tudor edifice, and the shiny grey Roller that was parked in front of the garage. His anger simmered again and his grip on the steering wheel became vice-like.

He sat for quite some minutes, just staring at the place, but then eventually turned the key to start his engine again, and drove away muttering under his breath, "You lecherous bastard Goulder, I've got your number."

He was home early for a change and Angie seemed quite surprised as he stepped inside and threw his coat onto the chair by the hall telephone.

"I thought you said you'd got something to attend to. I didn't really expect you home in time for dinner"

"Oh, it didn't take long", he replied without elaborating.

It had become quite unusual for them to eat together, in fact Angie never missed a chance to moan about his hours, whilst Mike was always of the opinion that the hours came with the job. A vocation wasn't something bound to a nine to five existence, a bit insensitive perhaps, but that's our Mike.

The television set was blaring out the tail end of the local area news and Mike sat back in his favourite arm chair to watch. Only the next moment, Angie was shaking him awake, telling him dinner was served. He must have been so tired, the moment he relaxed he'd fallen asleep. The small talk over dinner was of that day's presentation although Mike tried his best to avoid it, but Angie insisted on re-living her glamour appearance and the jealousy of her 'rivals'. Mike noticed that she was still dressed in her finery and asked,

"Are you going out somewhere tonight?"

"I've promised to meet Janice – you know, Janice Thomas – I didn't expect you home. I've not seen Janice for such a long time and we want to catch up. You don't mind do you?"

"I don't suppose it'd matter if I did mind. What time are you going to be back?"

"Oh, I don't know. I don't expect to be late, but if you're home you needn't wait up".

No more was said and Mike returned to his arm chair and the television. It wasn't long before he was dozing once again and the next thing that he heard was the bang of the door as Angie left.

The television continued to play to itself as Mike was too preoccupied in his own thoughts to pay it any attention. Angie was going out with her friends too regularly for his liking, and going to extraordinary lengths with her appearance each time.

He realised it wasn't healthy to harbour thoughts of infidelity, but for a while he thought of nothing else, and toyed with following Angie, but then dismissed the notion as paranoia. 'Paranoia, there's that same damned word again, paranoia', he thought, 'perhaps I am losing my marbles'. He picked up the newspaper and began to read but he couldn't concentrate and threw it to one side. He went through to the kitchen and began to make himself a cup of coffee, but the same thoughts kept crowding his mind, and he poured the coffee down the sink, grabbed his coat and fumbling for his car keys, went out the door leaving the lights on and the television playing.

Angie's Mini Cooper had gone. It was his present to her last year on her twenty-eighth birthday, and she loved her little car, although the silver metallic paint wasn't quite Mike's taste.

He set off towards the city but realised as he drove that he didn't actually know where Janice Thomas lived, just the general location. She wasn't one of his friends but someone Angie had known at college. Still, he'd recognise Angie's little car anywhere. Almost an hour passed, searching one street after another but there was no sign of Angie or the car. Mike pulled to the side and stopped as the 9.30pm London train, rattled into the nearby station. Whatever prompted him he couldn't say but he started the car again and drove into the railway station car park.

He drove down the avenue of parked cars – and there, right at the extreme, where the illumination was almost non-existent, was Angie's car. It was strange to say the least if she was visiting a girl friend that her car should be parked at the railway station, almost as though hidden away. It just confirmed in Mike's mind that she was cheating on him.

He settled to wait. The next two hours were tedious and cold and he had to keep running the engine to keep warm. Long hours of monotonous observation were nothing new to Mike but this was different and his mind raced with different scenarios. Perhaps there was some innocent explanation – then what? How was she going to react to him surreptitiously following her. Perhaps..., perhaps – damn it, there was no perhaps, she was cheating on him and he was going to find out with who.

Time dragged by but eventually the headlights of an approaching car swept fleetingly across his own vehicle. Mike slid down in his seat trying to make his car appear empty, and then as it passed he sat upright again to see that familiar grey Roller brake to a halt near Angie's car and extinguish all lights. It was dark and quite dismal but there was no mistaking Angie as she stepped from the Roller. She closed the passenger door, and as she waved her good-bye the lights came on again and it pulled away.

She looked after the Roller for a brief moment and then went to her own car. Mike stayed until Angie had driven away and then set off using all the short cuts he knew to get him home before she arrived.

He was sitting in front of the television as Angie's key turned in the lock.

"Hello, you still up?" she asked nonchalantly.

"Did you have a good evening with Janice?"

"Yes, we've had a good old natter. She's doing well for herself – she's running a free lance outfit making television programs. She seems to have married fairly well and they've two daughters. She's not promised me anything but she says there just might be an opening for me".

"Oh, very nice",

There wasn't much conviction in his voice in answering her and he rose to his feet and headed towards the stairs. He was in bed and had turned off the light before Angie joined him. His mind was in turmoil but he just had to hold his tongue. His back was turned and he ignored her as she snuggled up for warmth, but sleep didn't come easily for him.

Angie still slept as Mike rose with the dawn, shaved and left the house quietly. It was normal for Mike to be first in at the office, he'd always liked to have that early chance of being first to obtain the incoming information, and it gave him some 'quiet time' to compose himself and plan the day before the 'circus' began.

He switched on his computer screen and logged in. It always took a few moments to boot up and become accessible, so he occupied his time going through the written log left by the night shift. There was nothing interesting and so he returned to the computer screen and checked for messages and instructions – nothing.

His mind was still so unsettled thinking of Angie and his first thoughts were to search Google to see what it brought up regarding Janice Thomas – who the hell was she?. Was she just a fiction in Angie's mind to divert the truth? That drew a complete blank and he wondered was Janice Thomas her maiden name? He didn't know and he hadn't had the sense to quiz Angie, nor had he had the sense to ask about this outfit making television programs – surely that would have had a web site.

As a last despairing chance and thinking again about the Roller that had dropped off Angie at the Railway Station car park he typed in Herbert Goulder and clicked on 'search' The web site was only a brief affair with the usual smiling photograph and a resume of his political career with dates and times of his open surgery for contact, but never-the-less Mike ran off a copy on the printer. He folded the paper and slipped it into his jacket.

Chapter 3

A Chemistry Lesson.

There was a knock and Sergeant Ron Tasker popped his head around the half open office door.

"Hi Mike. I saw your car in the yard so I thought I'd catch you nice and early. You're due to re-qualify again on the range. When's it going to be convenient?"

Ron was uniform but he'd been around for ages and he was the number one firearms instructor for the force and his experience and firearms capabilities couldn't be questioned. He was one of the good guys

"I might as well come down with you now – if that's O.K. It's quiet and there's nothing burning so let's get it done with."

Putting the computer on 'stand-by', he grabbed his jacket and followed Sergeant Tasker to the lift. Ron pressed the button for the basement and said,

"There's a lot of talk about yesterday, Mike. Look, it's none of my business but, as a mate, I want to warn you – you know, to just watch out for yourself."

The lift jerked to a halt and they stepped out into a short subterranean, white painted, concrete tunnel, brightly lit by fluorescent tubes. Only a few short steps brought them to the hardened steel security gates which gave access to the armoury. Ron swiped his pass card and punched in the security numbers, and there was an audible 'click' as the lock released.

"Thank's all the same Ron, but I know what's being said. At least whilst they're talking about me they'll not be talking about anyone else."

The 'clang' of metal upon metal echoed in the corridor as the security gate closed behind them. Next, the electronic locks on the heavy metal door of the armoury itself, were released by Ron's number punching, and finally the more ordinary locks that responded to his key.

"It's better protected than Fort Knox", joked Mike.

"It sure is, but pity the poor bastard that loses his key or his swipe card…", responded Ron, "….There are cameras and alarms at every access point and when they go off the noise is deafening. It's happened to me, just once, and you never want it to happen again. You see, they can't be turned off down here, only in the control room up above, and all hell breaks loose. Even now we're being monitored on CCTV", and he pointed to the several cameras.

Mike laughed as together they selected the weapons. There were three grades of weapons to the qualification, first the Heckler & Koch MP5 9mm light machine carbine, the Browning and the Walther PPK 9mm automatic pistols, and then the Smith and Wesson .36 'Police Special' short barrelled revolver.

Things had developed quickly over the last few years as the police had been forced to respond to more and more sophisticated weapons that were available to the criminal and the terrorist. Mike reflected that only very recently, he and the other qualified firearms users, were entirely restricted to the Home Office approved 'Police Special' with its limited capacity. Only six chambers – and at that, one chamber was kept empty as a safety recommendation, and very often when firearms were issued, a maximum of ten rounds were issued per officer. Not much use against automatic weapons.

The Home Office and the Association of Chief Police Officers (ACPO) have woken up at last to the need for a more radical approach to the question of firearms training and availability. The sight of uniformed officers working in public areas such as air terminals, sporting light machine guns, is a sight to which we've all become accustomed over recent months, but to some it was a sight that was never anticipated in a million years.

The two officers entered the range and even though the outer safety gates were locked, the red warning light was illuminated outside the range, as a safety precaution.

"O.K. Mike, you know the drill, but we have to go through the procedure for each qualifier. So, if you have a malfunction, raise your arm and I'll come to you. There's a slight possibility of a misfire as all our range ammunition is re-loads, that's no problem, but always leave the weapon facing down the range. Never turn back towards me with a loaded weapon. I know, you've heard it all before but I have to repeat it with everyone who uses the range."

Continuing he said, "You can take as long as you wish to accustom yourself with the weapon and get your eye in, then, as soon as you're ready, signal to me and I'll start the film. You know what's expected, this is a terrorist situation with hostages, and you are expected to use your own initiative and decide what is, and what is not, appropriate."

Pointing to the target area, he said,

"If you decide a particular scene is a "No Shoot", perhaps because someone, a hostage maybe, is in the line of fire, then you must shout "No Shoot". The same applies if the terrorists are trying to surrender. However, your marks will be governed by the target scores and your ability to differentiate between "Shoot" and "No Shoot" situations. Indicate when you're ready to start".

Mike took little time to accustom himself with the weapon, he switched on his "ready" light and the film began. Whoever had made that film and synchronised it with the moving targets had Mike's admiration, it was quite the best he'd seen and it all appeared so realistic.

When it was over and all the weapons had been fired the range was cleared and Mike went back to the armoury for his practical test on assembly and disassembly of the weapons.

At the end Roy brought in the test sheets and together they went through them.

"It's a high percentage pass Mike. There's just one thing that I've criticised you for – it's something you need to bear in mind; that's hesitation. There were a couple of "Shoot" scenarios where you were a bit hesitant and you know hesitation can be fatal. Other than that it was good and you've re-qualified".

By the time he got back to the office it was the usual daily pandemonium with all the shouting and frustration of an office. Andrew Parr was the first to notice Mike's arrival and sat on Mike's desk to address him.

"Mike, the gaffer wants us in his office. He's got something up his sleeve".

The "gaffer" as Andy referred to was in fact the Detective Inspector, James Johnson.

"Does he just want the two of us?"

"As far as I know. He didn't say much, just asked me to tell you".

The door was wide open as Mike and Andy approached. Jimmy looked up from his paperwork and dropped his pen on the desk.

"Come in and Shut the door behind you Andy. Grab a seat". He leant back in his chair and lit a cigarette. There was nearly always a cigarette smouldering away on the ash-tray, he didn't seem to smoke a great deal – probably didn't have the time – but the smoke of the smouldering cigarette always caught on Mike's throat whenever he entered Jimmy's room. The introduction of legislation regarding smoking in the workplace wasn't even considered yet.

"I don't know what we've got – perhaps nothing at all – but it's something we've got to take a look at. It's confidential information from an industrial chemist regarding two men that approached him in a pub and began to quiz him about explosive substances. There was nothing specific about it and he wasn't asked to supply anything, but he was very uneasy about it and decided to report it".

Andy asked, "Do we know who they were 'Boss'? Or what pub this was?"

"We don't know who they are but the chemist had got the sense to watch them as they left and he took the registration number of their vehicle. We're checking that out at this very moment. The pub was the Wheatsheaf on Grange Road, near the university."

"How do you want us to approach this, Boss? Presumably we're going to identify these two from the registration number, so do you want a direct approach?" asked Andy.

"No. Let's not rush into this until we know what we've got. First of all I want you to interview this chemist and get a full statement from him about the men. Their descriptions, what they talked about, the car, etc. Anything that you think might be relevant, but do try to get him to give you some idea as to what they wanted the information for, and whether they seemed to have any practical knowledge about explosives. We want to know whether they were regulars in that pub and whether he'd ever seen them before"

"O.K. Boss, we'll do our best", said Mike as they rose and left the office.

Andy read the information sheet aloud as they walked back to the general office.

"Doctor Ali Ahmad Rajavi, Phd., MChem., Fellow of the Royal Institute of Chemistry, employed in Grayscale Bio-Chem plc, and associate of Crenarth University. Hmm.. some title".

"O.K. Get on the 'phone to Grayscale Bio-Chem – make us an urgent appointment with our Doctor Ali" said Mike.

Within minutes of Andy's request for an appointment, Dr.Rajavi was on the 'phone.

"Look, this is a very sensitive matter, I'd rather that we kept our interview secret from the staff here. Meet me in the café opposite the central railway station in thirty minutes"

'The One Stop Cafeteria – All day breakfasts', read the sign. It was busy as usual, plenty of customers from the railway station and the 'bus terminal, people who hadn't much time to wait about. As a table became vacant, a youngster in uniform check shirt and black trousers was there to remove the debris and wipe the surface clean. It wasn't a very 'up market' place, but quite clean and the food and prices were quite reasonable. Mike spotted a vacant table near the door where they could easily watch for Dr. Ali's arrival, and he took a corner chair. Andy took a tray and joined the queue at the counter.

Doctor Rajavi was easy to recognise as he pushed open the door. He was about forty- five and had the neat black hair and swarthy appearance of the Middle East, just as Mike had anticipated. He was dressed in a dark grey pin-striped suit, and his slim figure and smart appearance gave him the appearance of some office executive. He looked around as he entered the café and immediately caught Mike's eye. As he approached the table Mike rose and offered his hand, "Doctor Rajavi?" and as the doctor affirmed, Mike introduced himself.

No sooner were they seated than Andy was back with three cups of tea.

"Forgive me for saying this doctor, but your English is perfect – no trace of any foreign accent", said Mike.

"I'm second generation British…", laughed Dr Rajavi. "…My grandparents came here from Persia in the early nineteen thirties, my father was born here and married an English girl". Mike smiled and nodded his head in understanding.

"Let's get down to business. You've reported this suspicious incident. Would you like to repeat what you saw?" said Mike as he produced a small recording device that he placed on the table in front of Doctor Rajavi.

"Yes, certainly. Two evenings ago, I had left the office at about 6.30pm but I had to return for a meeting at 8.30pm. It wasn't really worth rushing home and then rushing back, so I did what I normally do, I go along to the local pub, The Wheatsheaf, where I can grab a bite and a coffee with time to spare. I sat in a corner seat reading a magazine whilst I ate. I saw two men come to the bar – whether they were already in the pub, or whether they came in from outside, I don't know." He hesitated to take sip of tea before continuing.

"What attracted my attention was their accents. It seemed a familiar sound, much like my grandfather's accent. Anyway, they carried their drink to a table near mine – they were drinking soft drinks. I'd guessed they were Iranian from their appearance and accent. After a short while they engaged me in conversation and I quickly realised they knew exactly who I was. They said they'd attended my lectures at the university where I'm often engaged to speak; they were young enough to have been students – early twenties - but, quite honestly, I don't know whether that's an accurate assessment.". He paused and shook his head side to side.

"I certainly didn't recognise either of them. Their conversation quickly became specific in questioning me about my work with Grayscale Bio-Chem. I tried to turn the conversation around by asking them what their interest in chemistry was but I couldn't get them to elaborate. The most that I could get from them was that they shared an amateur interest in chemistry. I don't know why, perhaps it was their reluctance to give a straight answer, but I began to get very suspicious of them".

"You said something about their interest in explosives…", said Andy, "…Can you elaborate?"

"Yes, that's correct. As I said, I was already getting very suspicious of them, and I made an excuse that I must leave to attend a conference. The fact that I was about to leave seemed to make them concentrate their questioning on their real purpose. One of them asked me where he could obtain 30% concentrate hydrogen peroxide. That really started the alarm bells ringing so I made my excuse and left quickly without giving an answer".

"Why, what's significant about 30% hydrogen peroxide ?" asked Mike.

"Well, to anyone who knows the most basic chemistry, that's one of the crucial elements in making HMTD – a very powerful explosive", replied the doctor.
Andy looked confused,

"What was that, HMTD ?

"Hexamethylene triperoxide diamine, HMTD. It's what they call an organic chemical compound, a high explosive that's easy to produce with the most basic of equipment and all the elements are easy to obtain. Anyone with even the most basic knowledge of chemistry can make it and that's what makes it such an attractive explosive to terrorists." Taking another sip of tea he continued,

"You asked me what was significant about 30% strength hydrogen peroxide. It's used for many purposes – quite legitimate purposes such as lady's hairdressing for hair bleach, but at a much lower strength. Thirty to thirty-five per cent strength is the optimum in making the explosive. The only other ingredients that are needed are Hexamethylenetetramine – which is the solid fuel tablets for campers that are available at any army surplus stores – and a small quantity of citric acid".

The doctor paused to see that Mike and Andy were absorbing what he was saying, as he finished his tea.

"I want you to understand that this is a very, very powerful explosive that is extremely dangerous to everyone – most of all to those who try to manufacture it. It's very unstable. The slightest friction, shock, heat, etc, will all set off an explosion. Contact with metal causes a reaction and metal containers and even metal instruments used in the mixing process can cause it to explode. Even sun light will do it – I can't stress enough, it's very, very sensitive. If any of your men come into contact with this compound, they must leave it alone and let someone deal with it who knows what they are doing".

"That's all very interesting and a bit alarming..." said Mike, "….but what makes you so suspicious of these men? What makes you think that their intention was to produce that explosive?"

"It's just a gut feeling, but why would anyone with a legitimate purpose come to question me about how to obtain such chemicals? We all hear so much about terrorism these days and I feel we've all got a responsibility to be alert to such a threat".

"Is this stuff, this HMTD, what they call 'The Mother of Satan?… ", asked Andy, "…I've heard plenty about terrorists using that".

"No, that's Triacetone Triperoxide – TATP. It's another easily produced explosive, but it's even more dangerous to produce than HMTD. It was something that was used a lot by the Palestinians against the Israelis and you could identify the bomb makers because they'd nearly all lost a hand in making it. HMTD is almost as dangerous to produce but there's always going to be those fanatics who'll risk the loss of a limb, or even life itself, in their cause."

"You said earlier that when you became concerned about them you made an excuse and left, but your initial report also said that you'd watched them leave and you took down the registered number of the vehicle", said Mike.

"Yes, I went outside but I concealed myself in the car park and watched as they climbed into a car driven by a third man who appeared to have been waiting for them. It was an old dark green Rover – I know it was a Rover because I used to own one myself. The only trouble is I had nothing to hand to write down the number and had to commit it to memory. I know it was 'TRV 881' but I'm unsure of the last letter. I think it was 'M' but I'm not absolutely sure".

"Right doctor, we've got a picture of what transpired. We've got to get back and digest this to see where it takes us. We shall be back in touch with you to keep you informed of progress", said Mike.

"I'll give you my business card, that's got my mobile number on it. I'd prefer that you use that and then I can keep this secret – you know what office gossip is like", said Dr. Rajavi.

Mike seemed to be contemplating something and sat for some moments in quiet thought before he said,

"You're obviously very qualified and knowledgeable in this field, do I detect something of a specialist nature about you in Middle East affairs?"

"Yes, you're quite right. Very perceptive of you. I spent some time in the Middle East – Jordan, Iran and Iraq – prior to the Iran-Iraq war in 1986. I was ostensibly working for Grayscale but both the British and American military used my insight into the politics and pressures of the areas. I've maintained that interest in the Middle East since I returned to this country in 1993, but apart from just one or two instances since then, the military haven't needed my input".

"Oh, just one more thing before we go. Can you think of any reason that they should pick you out – that is apart from your connection with the university?", asked Mike.

"I've thought long and hard about that and really it's all speculation but the thought did cross my mind that they associated my name with someone with a notorious reputation. They were a husband and wife partnership, Massoud and Maryam Rajavi. They're no relation to my family, it's simply a coincidence in the surname." He waited whilst an employee of the cafe collected empty cups, then continued,

"I was telling you about Massoud and Maryam Rajavi. They were a part of a terrorist group called the 'People's Mujahedin of Iran' or the 'National Liberation Army of Iran'. –It was also known by the acronym PMOI or MEK and MKO, and was formed a long time ago. It was devoted to the armed struggle against the then Shah of Iran, but it also became opposed to Western Imperialism and capitalism in general. I can tell you a lot more about them but I won't bore you with all that now. As I said, that connection is pure speculation, but I did initially think they'd formed that association with my name".

Mike turned off his recording device and placed it in his pocket, and as they rose from the table Mike extended his hand to Dr. Rajavi and said,

"Thank's for your help with this. I'll be in touch with you very soon.

Back at the office Mike and Andy went straight to the DI's office. The door was wide open and Jimmy sat at his desk. The smoke haze from the cigarette burning away in the ash-tray, hung heavily in the room. He looked up as Mike gave a cursory tap on the open door as he walked into the office.

"Well, how did you get on?" Jimmy asked.

"The truth is..." answered Mike, "...I don't know what we've got. The guy who reported this, Doctor Rajavi, is as good a witness as you're ever likely to get. He's a sound guy. He knows all there is to know about explosives but he's also something of an expert on Middle East affairs. He's British through and through although he's of Persian extraction, and he's worked with the military in the Middle East. I've recorded our interview and I'd like you to hear what he says – so you can make your own mind up." He fumbled in his pocket for the recording device which he placed on the table before he continued,

" My own personal opinion is that he was right to be suspicious of these men, but there's nothing solid that we can act upon".

Jimmy picked up the internal telephone and dialled. It was quite obvious he was talking to Detective Superintendent Birchall even though only Christian names were being used.

"Alan, if you can spare us a minute or two I'd like you to listen to what we've got. It could be something quite serious".

As he put the 'phone down he rose and stubbed out the half burnt cigarette, and said, "Come on, he wants us in his office right now – and Mike, bring that recording with you."

The green "Enter" light flashed on the door pillar of Detective Superintendent Birchall's office, so Jimmy knocked and led the way in.

"What have you got for me Jimmy?" asked Birchall.

"Well, it's information that we've received from a member of the public. He's a chemist, but he's also very savvy to what's happening around the Middle East, and he's someone the military have used in the past – so he's someone to take notice of. Mike has a recording of the interview that I want you to listen to and I understand it's self explanatory", said Jimmy.

He turned to Mike in expectation as Mike produced the recording device from his pocket. The four of them sat in silence as the recording was played.

"He's quite positive they were pumping him for information about bomb making ingredients isn't he?" said Birchall after listening to the recording, more as a statement than a question.

"He is Guv…" answered Mike, "….He's firmly of the opinion that we have an active terrorist cell on our patch."

"Well, what can we do to identify them?"

"I suppose the first thing is work on that registration number that he gave us. He wasn't sure about the last letter but he knew that it was an old Rover. If the rest of the number is correct then it shouldn't be beyond us to figure out the correct registration", said the Detective Inspector.

"I suggest that we put someone on to Doctor Rajavi – it'll have to be with his knowledge and approval of course – to watch for any further contact", said Andy.

"That'll be a bit awkward…..", countered Mike, "……because he wants it kept from his office staff in case there could be an 'inside' connection."

"Well, they obviously knew him, and therefore they could find him in the telephone directory, and could ring him at home. I suggest we could have his line monitored", said Jimmy.

"Again, it'd have to be with his consent", said Birchall.

"Has anyone thought of the university connection? – if he's correct about the Iranian accent then surely the university would have a record of Iranian students", volunteered Andy.

"It's worth a try…", said Mike "….but how far back do we go in their records?"

"Well, if we take it on face value, and take into account what Doctor Rajavi said, the suggestion was that they had attended one of his lectures. It seems reasonable to assume that only those students with an interest in chemistry and physics would have attended his lectures – so if we go back five years and identify Iranian students with a chemistry connection that could give us a start", answered Jimmy.

"I agree with that…", said Birchall, "….but I still think that the vehicle number gives us our best lead."
Birchall picked up the plastic 'No Smoking' sign and tapped it lightly on the desk top. Jimmy took the hint and replaced the packet of cigarettes in his pocket. "Sorry sir, force of habit", he said apologetically.

"O.K. then. I want you Mike, to write up a comprehensive report and I need it on my desk within an hour. I need to contact the counter terrorism desk at both the Security Service and the Met. They'll need a copy of your report faxing to them as soon as possible. We're going to have them running all over us in the next day or so and so we need to get busy and follow any leads that we can before they get here. We don't want to look like a bunch of idiots do we? I'll speak to the ACC and explain the situation", said Birchall.

The ACC Michael Coverly responded very positively to Birchall's information.

"This is obviously going to be a difficult business. I want you to include the CID, do whatever's necessary. Pull all the detectives off all the non-urgent stuff to concentrate on this. They've got their informants – tell them to put some pressure on – we need to find these people, and quickly. Haven't you got anyone in the Asian community? Get your own agents involved; make them earn their money. Speak to the Met – the Counter Terrorism Squad – and get their help if you think it's necessary. You know the drill Alan. Just keep me informed."

"Yes sir…" responded Birchall, "...It's already in hand to speak to the Met and the Security Service but I wanted your approval first."

Mike returned to his desk and struck up the computer. As he waited to log on, he picked up the small silver framed photograph of Angie from his desk. He was lost in thought again for some moments, immersed in his own personal problems, but then returned to the task in hand as the screen 'bleeped' at him. Pushing those problems to the back of his mind he began to rattle out his report on the keyboard.

Chapter 4

The Post Mortem

Angie rose from her chair, tossing the magazine onto the coffee table, as she heard Mike's key turn in the door.

"Oh, you do know where you live then?", was her sarcastic jibe but Mike felt too drained, too tired, to offer any response.

"Have you eaten?", she enquired, but Mike merely shook his head.

"O.K. I'll get something."

Mike slumped into his armchair and clicked the remote to bring on the television but after channel hopping for a moment or so, he clicked the stand-by button having found nothing that interested him. He lay back in his chair and closed his eyes. His head was swimming with the day's events.

Angie brought him a mug of his favourite coffee and he sat up to take it but offered no "thank-you."

"Mike, what's happening to us?"

"What do you mean? – 'what's happening to us?' ", he responded, taking a sip from his coffee.

"Well, there's obviously something going on. You're as distant and as cold as it's possible to be", she probed.

"Something going on?", he echoed, feeling his temper rise, but he 'bit his tongue' realising he wouldn't help the situation by venting his feelings.

"It's this damned job of yours isn't it? You never know when to come home. You carry all your worries in your head, and then when you do come home you're always so damned tired and short tempered. We never talk. There's lots of things I want to discuss with you, but I never get the chance. Can't you see, it's driving a wedge between us?"

Mike sat in contemplation for some moments without saying anything, but then responded,

"Look Angie, It's been a long day. You knew all about the hours when you married me. It's a good job, frustrating sometimes especially when you're dealing with idiots who think that in some way they're superior in both intellect and ability, but it's never been any different, and that I can cope with. I know you're left on your own for long hours, but there's very little I can do about that."

"Well, at least it's got us talking. I hate it when you're sullen and uncommunicative – especially when you turn your back on me in bed. It's hurtful…", said Angie, "...Let's try to get on. These last few hours I've thought we were heading for divorce."

"I'm sorry Angie. I've a lot on my mind at the moment", replied Mike still keeping his internal turmoil about her probable infidelity to himself.

"It's time you learned to leave your job behind, at the office, instead of bringing it home with you. You don't even share your problems with me, you just bottle things up inside. There's no wonder you seem so sullen to everyone."

As they sat down to eat, Mike said,

"You said something about there being lots of things you wanted to discuss – what things?"

He seemed to be just picking at his food.

"What's the matter? Is the ham 'off '?"

"No. It's fine. The truth is my appetite isn't what it could be…", he answered, "…What is it you want to discuss?"

"It's nothing much really. Little things take on much more importance when you're all alone and depressed. I was going to ask how you felt about me applying for this job with Janice Thomas? It's a bit of a dog's body's job – doing a bit of everything. There'll be a lot of clerical work and I suppose I shall be mashing tea for everyone, but that doesn't bother me – I'd be on the inside and I'd have a chance to learn all about the business. Who knows what it might lead to?"

"Well, if it's what you want, then go ahead, but who is this Janice Thomas. Do you know anything about this business she runs – like is it 'legit' ?"

He was still picking at his salad as Angie replied,

"I've told you before, I was at college with Janice and she runs a television advertising business. She still uses her maiden name – Thomas – for professional reasons but her married name is Goulder."

The alarm bells suddenly started to ring in Mike's mind,

"Goulder?" he asked suddenly bringing to mind the shiny grey 'Roller' that dropped Angie off at the railway station car park and the secluded spot where she had left her car.

"Yes, Goulder. You know, her husband's the City Councillor – the chairman of the Police Authority who presented the citations and commendations".

"Yes, Yes. I know who Goulder is – the lecherous bastard." The bitterness was quite palpable.

"What makes you hate him so? He's always seemed quite nice to me although I've not had much to do with him, you see he doesn't have anything to do with Janice's business."

"I'll bet" said Mike to himself under his breath. Suddenly the 'beep, beep' of his pager stopped the conversation.

Detective Superintendent Birchall's number was ingrained in Mike's memory and he tapped it into his mobile in an almost automatic manner.

"Yes, Guv. You paged me?"

"We've had a suspicious death Mike. It's unclear at the moment what's happened but uniform are dealing with a burnt out car that contained a body. Forensic are taking a look at it but first impressions are that the body shows signs of having died before the car fire. There's substantial damage to the head and one hand's missing. It looks for all the world like damage caused by an explosion and I think it might be connected with our enquiry."

"That sounds very likely, Guv. What do you want me to do?"

"Well, there's very little good we can do at this time of night… (Mike instinctively looked at his watch – the time was 10.20pm)…. so what I want you to do is meet me at 8.30am in the morning – at the office, and we'll have a look at the site of the burnt out car. Uniform have preserved the scene for us. Scenes-of-Crime officers have already examined it but I want them to go back with us, to have another look."

"O.K. Guv. Has there been any identification of the body?"

"No. That's a forensic job. You'll understand when you see the state of him. He's going nowhere – he's in the mortuary."

"O.K. Guv, see you at eight thirty", said Mike and he shut down his mobile connection.

"What was all that about?" asked Angie. Mike gave her the general outline of the conversation and she asked in an almost resigned manner,

"Does that mean you're going out again?"

"No. The Boss has asked me to meet him early tomorrow to have a look at it."

"Thank goodness for that, at least we can have one evening together. I'll get the coffee". That night Mike wasn't exactly amorous but there was a small degree of warmth between them, and they slept entwined as times past.

Mike rolled into the yard of headquarters within minutes of Alan Birchall who was already waiting. He was in conversation with a white coated Scenes-of-Crime officer and a uniform inspector.

"Mornin' Guv", said Mike, nodding affably to the others.

"Mike, this is inspector Allen from 'C' Division. He's the one who called this in. He thought there was more to this than met the eye – he's coming with us. We'll go in my car and SOCO will follow in his van."

The journey took them a considerable distance towards the outskirts of the city to an area of semi derelict ground that had probably remained a bombed out area since the nineteen-forties. There, behind mounds of broken masonry and other debris that had been tipped through the years, was the burned out shell, guarded by a uniform constable. Before they approached the vehicle, inspector Allen, explained,

"When my lads got here, it was still smouldering and they found the remains of a plastic container – most of which was burnt away, but I suspect had carried the petrol to douse the car and the body before setting fire to it. As you can see the number plates have been removed, as has the plate, with the VIN number, from the engine compartment."

The SOCO (Scene of Crime Officer) joined them as they viewed the burned out shell.

"What can you tell us?" asked Birchall.

"Well, there's no easy identification of either the body or the motor vehicle. I think it's probably and old model Rover. All the glass has gone but I've found some chassis markings and there's a number stamped into the engine block, so now someone can chase that up with the manufacturers. I've taken ash samples from inside the car body and forensics will be able to identify the agent used to cause the fire – most probably petrol.. The body had nothing on it, like rings or wrist watch, and the burning of the remaining hand was so severe that there's no possibility of fingerprints being taken."

"O.K. Have you taken plenty of photographs".

"Yes. I've taken all aspects of the car, both prior to the removal of the body and afterwards. I've also taken photographs of the body both in situ and at the mortuary. I've got photos of the site in general and the approach from the road."

"What about tyre tracks of other vehicles? Whoever burned this vehicle and dumped the body almost certainly left in another vehicle." said Mike.

"No, sorry. I've examined the whole of the site and unfortunately the ground is so hard there are no marks of any other vehicle".

"O.K. It seems as though you've been as thorough as you can be", said Birchall, then turning to Inspector Allen again, he continued,

"I want you to have this vehicle lifted and taken to headquarters and I'll get someone from the lab to come out and give it the once over."

"Oh, one more thing", Birchall said, addressing the SOCO, "Take soil samples from under the vehicle and also take some from nearby as control samples. I don't know what good it will do but I don't want to miss anything."
After a last careful look around the shell and the site, they left, leaving the SOCO to take his further samples for the H.O Forensic Science Lab.

Back at headquarters Birchall dropped off Inspector Allen with instructions to ensure that a copy of the file, including all statements of the officers who found the car, and anything material to the enquiry was forwarded to him.

"Get in touch with the 'Stolen Vehicle' squad, they'll give you some help in tracing those chassis and engine numbers. I want you to organise house-to-house enquiries around the site to see if we can find any witnesses. It's a remote chance but we can't ignore it."

Inspector Allen gave his assurance that the necessary enquiries would be made. Birchall drove off again.

"Where we goin' now Guv?" asked Mike.

"To the mortuary. Get on your mobile and ask someone back at the office to get in touch with the Forensic Science Lab and ask them to send someone out to the mortuary as quickly as possible to examine the body. I want DNA testing and a dental cast – just tell them to treat it as a murder enquiry – they'll know what to do."

Routine meant examination of the body by the Home Office Pathologist instead of the local pathologist who dealt with all the 'sudden deaths' occurring day by day where there was no suspicion of foul play. To avoid loss of vital forensic evidence he readily agreed to a scientist from the Forensic Science Lab to be present at the post mortem.

Facilities in this 'state-of-the-art' mortuary were quite excellent – far removed from only a few years back when post mortem examinations were carried out on a metal tray over an open drain. This mortuary was more akin to the excellence of a hospital operating theatre with all the intense lighting, extractor fans, electrical vacuum pumps, saws, etc.

The Home Office Forensic Scientist was first to examine the body, after all she was only concerned with extraneous materials, such as contained under the fingernails of the remaining left hand. The matter of removal of skin tissue and dental casts could be attended to after the post mortem.

Mr. Henderson, the renowned Home Office Pathologist, pulled the microphone down on its extending cable to a working height above the body, and dressed in his red ochre coloured rubber apron and gloves, he spoke into the microphone. After identifying himself and relating his very auspicious qualifications, he next identified those present.

"The cadaver is an unknown male. It's identified to me by Constable (881) Jackson who remains as observer. I am assisted by Doctor Helen Gray of the Crenarth Home Office Forensic Science Laboratory, and Mortuary Technician Mr

Harry James. Other observers present are Detective Superintendent Birchall and Detective Sergeant Borman.

"The whole body is extremely charred having been exposed to fire. However there are obvious physical injuries that do not relate to the fire. The head shows signs of severe trauma – the anterior section of the skull is severely depressed. The glabella around the right eye socket is macerated and the right cheek is also depressed. The right arm has suffered severe trauma and the forearm and hand are missing. Upon examination the limb appears to have been torn away. The body is otherwise intact. My initial thoughts are that the body was subject to a severe explosion."

"I shall begin my examination by removing the remains of the cranium. Using a scalpel I am cutting around the cranium at the forehead and around both sides above the ears. I am peeling back the scalp to reveal the cranium and using an electrical vibrating saw to remove the cranium to reveal the brain." He hesitated to peer closely at the tissue.

"I can see that there's extensive damage to the brain from the frontal lobe and anterior centre through to the right temporal lobe to a point above the ear. I am quite confident that this injury alone would have been fatal. There are signs of bruising and residual bleeding into the occipital region and cerebellum. I am now replacing the cranium, having secured samples for histology, and am pulling the scalp back into position."

"I shall next make an incision down the front of the chest and continue down the abdomen. I'm cutting the rib cage with secateurs and once removed I shall examine the lungs." He stopped momentarily to let Doctor Gray see the state of the lungs before continuing.

"My examination of both lungs shows no indication of smoke inhalation, and both are pink and healthy. The heart is that of a young man and shows no indication of cardiac disease. The stomach is now open and samples are taken. The remaining viscera reveal nothing of interest. The lower body is intact and shows no sign of damage other than by fire."

"My conclusion at this stage is that death was directly due to the damage to the brain. That damage could be consistent with some sort of explosion but equally may be unrelated.. The fire damage was quite definitely following death as the lungs were healthy and showed no signs of smoke inhalation."

"My findings, which are of course dependant upon histology, are that death was due to severe trauma to the brain. Report concluded."

Alan Birchall stepped forward as Mr. Henderson proceeded to scrub down and strip off the apron and gloves.

"Thank you Mr. Henderson. Can I offer you some hospitality at the local hostelry?"

Henderson laughed aloud,

"It's very tempting but I must decline. A while ago I would gladly have accepted but it's too risky now. The breathalyser has put paid to all that. Anyway, I have another appointment so I'll take my leave, but thank you all the same".

They shook hands and Henderson left.

Turning his attention to Doctor Gray, Birchall said,

"What can we do to help you?"

"Nothing thank you. I have my blood samples and stomach contents for toxology and DNA testing. I now need to take a sample of skin to test for the explosives and then, all that remains, is a dental cast and the technician here will help me with that."   "O.K. I guess you're fed up of being asked this question, but how soon can we expect your report?" asked Birchall.

Doctor Gray gave a little chuckle and replied,

"It'll take a day or two before all my tests are complete but I can appreciate your urgency so I promise to telephone you as soon as I have anything, then you'll get my report through the normal channels."

"O.K. doctor. Well, thank you. We'll leave you to get on with your work", said Birchall and he shook hands and left. As they walked outside into the fresh air, Mike took a deep breath and shook his head,

"Bloody hell, Guv. I'm glad we don't have to go through that every day. I hate mortuaries, particularly the smells. You never get used to the gasses from bodies as they're cut open, and they all seem to use that same disinfectant that smells of freesias - I hate it. It clings to your clothes and you smell it for hours afterwards."

"No, it's not my favourite past-time either. I suppose I'd better check that uniform have been in touch with the Coroner – there'll have to be an inquest. Come on, let's get back to the office, I must update the ACC and I've lots of 'phone calls to make.

Chapter 5

Counter Terrorism

The old warehouse had seen better days but the space it offered for the film and advertising business was ideal for Janice and her crew. She'd invested a fair amount of both time and effort inside the building. The office accommodation was 'high tech' with the latest computerised software that any self respecting film company would be proud of, and the space provided by this warehouse made possible several studios in which differing 'mock-up' scenes could be left in place.

Janice had surrounded herself with technicians and camera men that already had the experience of years with other established companies and who were looking for a new challenge in their careers.

Such a man was Tariq Jamil, a rather suave 50 years old with those sophisticated Middle Eastern looks that reminded one of the film star and professional bridge player, Omar Sharif. His silvering hair emphasised his looks and Janice had immediately taken to Tariq with a clear intention to use his looks and charm in fronting her programs. However Tariq had other ideas and knew his greatest assets lay behind the camera lens, not as a camera-man but a producer and fixer.

The informal meetings where ideas were formulated and thrashed out, and budgets discussed and mainly discarded, usually took place around packing cases outside the office, away from the telephones and computers that were a distraction.

The place wasn't exactly warm even in the height of summer, but now as the days grew shorter there was a real chill about the place. The coffee steamed in the cool air.

"Tariq, How goes your project?" asked Janice.

"We're no further than the planning stage at this moment."

"Well, just run through it for me. Give me some idea of where you're going with it".

"O.K. Well, we all agreed that we needed something topical, and something that was going to grab attention, if it was ever going to sell. I suggested that because terrorism was on everyone's mind, and illegal immigration was a hot potato, something that incorporated the two subjects was bound to be good. Now, although terrorism's a good subject, terrorists aren't that easy to find, as you can imagine, so I've begun from the other angle – illegal immigrants.

"We're blessed with an ever growing number but it's almost a closed door – trying to get on the inside. They're mainly East Europeans, not really the sort to be involved in terrorism, and they're being run by 'gang-masters' who find them accommodation and convey them wholesale to whatever work they're doing. It's almost worth doing an exclusive on them alone because it's almost like organised slave labour." He looked at Janice to guage her reaction before continuing.

"So, although this side of the plan is still ongoing, and the enquiries are still being followed...", he continued, "...I've had to think again. It grieves me to say but terrorism is more likely to be the province of the zealots and radicals of extremist Islamic factions – so what better place to start than the mosque. Being Muslim I've been accepted at the central mosque and I'm cultivating the Imam", Tariq explained.

"So, the fact is we've nothing at the moment", said Janice. Her tone of voice didn't exactly inspire Tariq, but he continued undaunted.

"Correct. Although it's quite evident to me as a new-comer at the mosque, that there's a clear division between the older element and the youngsters. Quite a number of the younger men are showing an intolerant attitude to the pacifying views of the elders, and there is a tendency towards a rather radical interpretation of the teachings of Islam." He puffed out both cheeks before loudly exhaling,

"I was well prepared for a sympathetic attitude towards the hostiles in both Iraq and Afghanistan, but I didn't expect to find such a burning unrest amongst the youngsters here, regarding this subject. The vitriol towards Britain, and America in particular, is quite intense. It's convinced me that if I can keep going with my enquiries, we shall soon have something. I'll bring it to you as soon as I've got something so that we can devise a budget".

Janice flipped over the sheets of paper on her clip-board and said,

"Alright. Well all we can do with that is sit tight and wait."

"The "Thank you Tariq" she gave didn't seem to have any heartfelt conviction. She continued, "Now to pass on to something completely new, we've had a commitment from the Fairburn Sun-Block Company for a short commercial. I've got certain ideas of my own but I would like to discuss it first with our animators. I need something fairly quickly to put forward at our head to head with Fairburn's publicity department."

At that moment the office door opened and a young clerk poked his head through and shouted for Janice to answer the telephone and with that the meeting broke up.

Detective Superintendent Birchall allowed the pen to slip from his fingers in a moment of frustration as the telephone demanded to be answered. 'If only I could get through this paper work without interruption', he thought.

"Yes" he answered curtly.

"Is that Detective Superintendent Birchall?"

"Yes", was the frustrated reply.

"This is Commander Dennis of the Metropolitan Counter Terrorism Squad".

"Oh, my apologies. I'm sorry I was short – this telephone's the bane of my life".

"Are we on a secure line Superintendent?"

"Yes we are".

"I have a faxed copy of a report by your Detective Sergeant Borman. It's pretty obvious that you've something sinister going on there. Now, of course we're interested, but at the moment there doesn't seem much point in dispatching a squad to Crenarth. We're fairly stretched at the moment. If you keep us informed of any developments we'll keep you under review."

"Well, I'd better update you now. There have been developments that could have a bearing on this but we're awaiting confirmation from forensics. A body's been found in a burnt out car; a male who seems to have died from some sort of explosion causing severe damage to the head and it had also torn away the right hand and forearm. There's nothing to connect the two incidents but it seems likely they are connected. Whoever placed the body in that car tried to destroy the evidence by setting fire to it."

After giving the matter a second or two's thought, Commander Dennis replied,

"This puts rather a different light on things. We'll wait for the forensic results but then we'll send you a squad. We've got some very experienced officers and a well tried system to help in an enquiry like this. Keep me informed."

"Certainly. I'll be in touch the minute I get the results...", answered Birchall. "...I've also been in touch with the Counter terrorism Desk at the Security Service. They're doing a search through the known activists to give us some names that we might match up."

"Yes, O.K. We'd be doing that anyway. Keep me informed", Commander Dennis answered then finally severed the connection.

Birchall hastily replaced the telephone on its cradle and immediately picked up the internal 'phone alongside.

"Mike, slip into my office for a minute",

Mike left the computer on screen saver and quickly made his way to the Chief Superintendent's office. The door stood open and Mike just gave the usual cursory knock as he entered. Birchall looked up from his paper work as Mike said,

"You wanted me Guv?"

"Yes, I've just had a Commander Dennis on the 'phone from the Counter-Terrorism Squad at the Yard. I've updated him on your report and he's going to send a squad up here. I need to know exactly where we're at with the enquiries to date".

"Right Guv. Well I've just had Inspector Allen from 'C' Division on the blower. He's been on to the Coroner and an inquest has been arranged for Tuesday next at 10am. It'll only be a matter of opening it and adjourning until a later date to enable our enquiries. So that's that taken care of. He's chasing up the paper work including the statements from the uniform lads that dealt with the car fire. The Stolen Vehicle Squad are able to identify the model of car as a Rover – but we already knew that.

"They haven't got much further yet on the engine and chassis numbers even though we've supplied them with the partial registration that Dr. Ali gave us. It seems the problem is caused by the fact that the Rover company went into liquidation and the new owners are having difficulties tracing the old records. I've got the first folder of photographs from SOCO but they don't tell us much.

"We're still waiting for Helen Gray to contact us from the Forensic Science Lab with a full report but the interim information is that it was petrol that was used to burn out the car – that doesn't take us very far – but she's sent us a full description of the dental cast and I'm just about to circulate all divisions within Crenarth and all surrounding forces for dental practices to be visited. That just may bring something in, but that's about it at the moment. Oh, I've had all the available CCTV footage sent in and I'm doing a computer check on our Aliens Registration documents for possibles, the most I can get from that is names but I'm trying to cross-reference them against the list we've got from the university – it's just a jumble of names at the moment."

"You say you've got all the CCTV footage. I take it you've considered CCTV at petrol stations? We might just find something interesting there – you know, like someone filling a container".

"Yes Guv, that's all in hand."

"O.K. You seem to be on top of things Mike. Have you been back in touch with Dr. Ali to check with him?"

"No Guv. I'll get one of the lads on to that straight away."

"OK, we've got to pull the stops out with this Mike and be right up there on top of the job. We don't want to look a bunch of country bumpkins when the Met lads get here. If anything breaks, even the smallest thing, I want to know about it straight away. The ACC has just been in touch with me – he's setting up an incident room. The idea is that CID and uniform will be drafted in to treat this enquiry as if it was a straight forward murder. All the information that they gather will be sifted by us and the Met boys. We'll be left to continue our enquiries regarding possible terrorism connections."

"O.K. Guv but don't let them divulge anything about the connection with explosives or this could be counter-productive."

"No, we'll keep on top of that but we need them to do the leg work, the house to house enquiries and all the dental practices."

The telephone was ringing its shrill alarm as Mike returned to his desk and he snatched the handset from its cradle. "Borman", he identified himself.

"Hello Sergeant, it's Hollis in 'comms' here. I've got the local press on the 'phone enquiring about the body found in the burnt-out car. What can I tell them?"

"Oh, you'd better put them through to me, I'll deal with it."

"O.K. put your phone down and I'll patch him through to you."

Only a brief second or two passed before the 'phone rang again, by which time Mike had quickly gathered his thoughts.

"Detective Sergeant Borman."

"Hello Mike, Guy Palmer here, Crenarth Post and Times. You'll remember me surely? I was at the Crown Court with you, reporting on your case with the shooters."

"Yes, Guy, I remember you....", lied Mike, "....What can I do for you?"

"Well, we've picked up from the listings at the Coroner's office that there's an inquest next Tuesday on an unidentified body. What gives Mike? Nobody seems to want to say anything."

"Well, the fact is we're keeping it under wraps Guy. Now then, there might eventually be a story in this for you that'll hit the nationals. I can't elaborate on it at the moment but if you and I can reach some understanding we can help each other."

"In what way?"

"Well, if you was prepared to run a piece in your paper, on the lines of a mystery body and asking for information from the public that might identify him, then we'd be prepared to brief you on the wider aspects as an exclusive, as and when it was possible to release the information – what do you say?"

"That seems good to me. Are you going to give me a hint as to what it's all about?"

"No. All that I'm prepared to tell you at this stage is that it's a matter of public safety but you mustn't make any mention about that or our deal's off. Understand?"

"O.K. I understand, just give me some details and we'll go to press but you've got to stick to your promise to keep it exclusive for me."

Mike agreed and outlined what he wanted Palmer to print.

Within minutes Mike had returned to Chief Superintendent Birchall's office,

"Guv, I've sort of jumped the gun a bit. I appreciate that it's not my place to give press releases, but I've just had a local reporter on the 'phone. He's picked up on the body in the burnt-out car from the Coroner's Office and he's rang me to get a story. I've held back on the circumstances, I've not mentioned that the death followed an explosion that blew away parts of his body. What I've done is ask him just to run a story about the body being found and asking for public response to try to identify him. In return I've promised him that we'll keep it under wraps until were ready to release the story which will then be exclusive to him. I hope I've done right but if I hadn't done a deal with him he'd have run with a story that might have compromised the enquiry."

"Right. That's good thinking, but if you're asked, you checked with me first and I sanctioned it, headquarters can be quite sensitive – understand?"

"O.K. Guv, Thanks."

Chapter 6

The explanation.

The office was empty apart from Mike who was frankly in no hurry to rush off home. He sat forlornly at his desk lightly fingering
the photograph of Angie. He felt the emotion welling inside and his eyes were decidedly moist. There was no-one there to cause him embarrassment and for once his feelings were able to surface.

"Oh God, Angie, why are you doing this to me?"

The wretched despair he was feeling at the thoughts of losing her began to expand into ideas of retribution against Goulder. The wealth and position that Goulder enjoyed – despite the age difference – was obviously the attraction for her, and the thought was eating away at Mike. He was surprised at himself for the diabolical schemes that kept circulating in his mind.

Footsteps in the corridor outside the office suddenly brought Mike out of his reverie and he quickly drew his sleeve across his moist eyes and pushed the photograph to its usual place at the back of his desk top. The door opened and in stepped Birchall.

"Ah. It's you Mike. I could see the lights on and I thought I'd better check that the office wasn't left unlocked."

"Yes Guv, I've been using a bit of quiet time to go over this terrorism business – trying to see what we're missing."

"Do you fancy a drink Mike? Come on, let's call in the Carpenters for a half – it'll help you unwind. You're beginning to let this business weigh too heavy. Are you sure you're delegating enough of the work?"

"Oh yes, Guv. All the lads are doing their fair share."

"Well the strain's beginning to show in your face, Mike."

Mike kept his real concerns to himself and grabbed his jacket from the back of his chair following Birchall through the door. The heavy lock clicked shut behind them and Mike inserted his key to turn the dead-lock.

"Would you and Angie fancy coming round to our place for an evening?" asked Birchall as they walked to their cars.

"I don't know Guv. The fact is Angie's so tied up with this new job of hers, I never know when she's free."

"Well, bear it in mind and if she's got a free evening, just let me know. It'll not be anything fancy, something like a Chinese take-away and a few beers. It'll just be nice to have a quiet evening together, to relax and chat – I know my wife'd enjoy it. See you down at the Carpenters. We wont stay long – just a half."

Mike slipped the key into the lock. He could see well enough that Angie was out. Her mini was gone and the house was in darkness. He switched on the hall light and could immediately see through to the kitchen and the yellow 'post-it' note stuck to the fridge door.

"Dinner in oven – just needs a few minutes to warm it up. Gone to see Janice. Got my mobile if you need me. Love Ange."

The miserable mood still hung around his shoulders no matter how he tried to throw it off. Jealousy and insecurity in his marriage were creating havoc in his mind. The micro-wave pinged and the plate burned his fingers as he lifted it out. The lamb chop with mint sauce was a favourite and at any other time he'd relish the meal. He had to admit Angie could cook, but his appetite wasn't at its best and he picked at the food; his mind was elsewhere.

The television held no interest for him and he felt so restless he just couldn't sit about. He fumbled through his pockets and found his car keys, pulled the door to behind him and went to his car.

The indicators flashed as he pressed the 'unlock' button of the keyfob, illuminating the gloom around him. He opened the door and sat behind the wheel in the darkness whilst his mind swirled around deciding what he was going to do and where he was going.

After a considerable time sitting with his head bowed, almost resting on the steering wheel, and his fingers drumming a dirge to accompany his mood, he started the car and reversed onto the road.

The car seemed to be on auto-pilot as Mike drove along the brightly lit street at a miserable speed. A blast from a car horn behind him shook him and he swerved in towards his nearside as an impatient driver overtook.

"Get stuffed" said Mike sticking a finger up against the window to show his contempt. At least the little episode made him concentrate a little more on his driving.

Turning into the railway station car park, he slowly drove along the rows of parked vehicles to the furthest point where the lighting was dimmest; to the point where he'd found Angie's car parked the previous evening, but it wasn't there.

He sat for a minute or so wondering what to do next and the only things going through his mind were the thoughts of Goulder. His head pounded to the beat of a hammer on a blacksmith's anvil and he switched on the interior light whilst he delved into the centre console to find his box of paracetemol. He pressed two tablets from the foil strip and threw them into his mouth. With nothing to drink the tablets seemed to catch in his throat but he persevered and swallowed them.

Thoughts of Goulder filled his head as he drove from the car park. What could he do to get back at this marriage breaker? Disable his car?

He parked on what seemed an otherwise deserted street. Flicking the internal light switch completely 'off' to avoid lights as he open the door, Mike stepped out of the car. The chill of the evening air made him pull his coat around him and zip up the fastening whilst he stood for a while, leaning on the car roof and checking up and down the street for signs of movement. He certainly didn't want nosey strangers observing him for what he had in mind.

The wind rustled through the trees; trees that obscured much of the street lighting to Mike's benefit. He crossed over into the deep shadow of the garden hedge, continuously looking about him. He stopped for a moment to check again for movement. He could see Goulder's house, a large detached property, with a gravel surfaced driveway, and surrounded by manicured lawns.

The down-stairs lights were on in several rooms although it seemed the curtains were closed. A light shone from a small window upstairs. Mike's senses were on full alert and the adrenalin was beginning to flow through his veins; the feeling of nervous tension was almost a drug that he lived for. He checked and checked again and his eye caught sight of a sign almost directly above where he stood proclaiming "This is a NEIGHBOURHOOD WATCH area"; how ironic.

He turned in at the driveway of the house and immediately the noise of the gravel underfoot unsettled him. He stood absolutely still and checked around him again, listening intently for the slightest sound that would stand out against the rustle of the trees and bushes in the wind.

Carefully stepping off the gravelled drive, over the prim little flower border onto the lawn, he stealthily approached the house. He could see in the semi darkness that there were either four or five cars parked. Suddenly he was bathed in bright light from a 'sunburst' type lamp over the garage up ahead. Panic struck him as he was totally vulnerable and he made a quick dash for the cover of the bushes and stood perfectly still, waiting for someone to appear from the house. Seconds passed that seemed like hours but no-one stirred and he realised that there must be movement sensors that brought on the light.

His confidence gradually returned and he continued, keeping well amongst the shrubs and bushes, still fearing that someone may appear. The lamp still bathed the area and he could plainly see four parked vehicles, and nestling in the middle, a fifth car, Angie's silver metallic Mini Cooper. Was there a party going on?

The roller shutter doors of the detached garage were raised and Mike could see the Rolls parked inside. He moved to approach the garage just as the house door opposite, opened. Mike stepped back again into his cover as a suave looking middle aged, middle-eastern looking guy with silvering hair and the looks of Omar Sharif emerged, closing the door behind him.

The 'sunburst' light above the garage door bathed the area in bright light once more.

The man tossed the clip-board and papers he was carrying into the rear-most BMW, sank into the driver's seat and sat there for a moment. He seemed to be trying to operate his mobile 'phone but either there was no signal or no reply.

A sudden thought grabbed Mike and he reached into his pocket and pulled out his own mobile to check that it was definitely turned off. He'd berated others in his command when their mobile had suddenly announced to the world that they were there when every effort was being made to ensure concealment; and here he was having forgotten to take that precaution. He silently cursed himself.

The BMW started up and slowly reversed from the driveway, its headlights intensifying the illumination as it did so. Mike maintained his cover; remaining absolutely still. He tried desperately to control his breathing which sounded to him like the noise of some enormous animal that was breathing fire and he opened his mouth to lessen the noise in his head. His heart was pounding.

After only a short time the place was returned to darkness as the 'sunburst' switched itself off, and he felt more at ease – at least the unexpected flood of light had allowed him to see plainly the obstacles that lay in his way and the scene beyond. Furthermore he'd been able to see the movement-sensor above the garage doors, but there must have been another somewhere part way down the drive.

He eased his way to the side of the garage wall and then, being under the sensor and under its arc of coverage, was able to get into the open garage without triggering the light. The sweat was beginning to run down the side of his face, still uncertain what he was going to do, he tried the front passenger door of Goulder's Rolls Royce and it almost silently clicked open. The interior light seemed to flood the darkness of the garage so he quickly, but quietly, shut the door again.

After just a moment or two's thought, he slid out of the garage and along the house wall, making for the windows that were lit. First at one and then the next, he pressed himself against the window trying to find a gap in the curtains but he could see nothing and the double glazing made it impossible to hear anything. There was certainly no loud music or raucous laughing to be heard.

There was nothing to be achieved here and he felt more than a little exposed so he moved back to the garage.

No sooner had he reached it than the 'sunburst' flooded the garden again and there were several voices emerging from the house. Mike frantically sought somewhere to hide and found a corner where gardening tools were leaning against the wall and a long waterproof coat hung from a nail. He flattened himself to the wall and pulled the coat around him. Headlights lit up the garage as car engines started and the vehicles began to manoeuvre and leave to the shouts of "Bye" and "Cheerio". The thought suddenly struck Mike that Angie might see his car parked at the roadside as she left.

All eventually went quiet again but the 'sunburst' stayed lit and he daren't move until it switched off. He began to breathe more easily as the place returned to darkness. His mind raced and he found himself asking the question, 'What the hell am I doing here? What have I achieved apart from risking everything?'

He unwrapped himself from the coat and began to move but his foot caught against something and a sudden deafening clatter filled the garage. He bent down and fumbled on the floor to find a spade had fallen. His heart almost stopped but no-one seemed to have heard and he quickly left the garage for the bushes again. He made his way down the lawn, keeping well clear of the driveway and the possible sensor, and out onto the street. He reached the car and turned for home.

"Good grief Mike, look at your shoes – take 'em off...", was Angie's response as he entered the house. " Where've you been? You look as though you've been dragged through a hedge."

"Oh, it's been an observation job..." he responded dismissively, "...Have you had a good evening?", he enquired with suspicion still filling his mind.

"Yes, we've had a meeting at Janice's house. They've got several things on the go but we've been finalising some advertising footage with the publicity agent for a sun-block company.

Angie's explanation somehow took the steam out of Mike's suspicions – everything seemed to fit what he'd seen.

"Was Goulder there?"

"I think so. Janice said something about him being upstairs in his office, why? What makes you so concerned about him?"

"Oh, it's nothing really. I just don't like him."

"Have you eaten – shall I get some supper?"

"No. I'll just have a drink – I need to take some tablets, I've had a blinding headache all evening".

"Mike, you don't look well. It's time you saw your doctor. Shall I make you an appointment?" Mike just shook his head.

After two more pain killers with his cup of tea Mike left Angie reading some typed A4 sheets, and went upstairs. Throwing his clothes onto the chair beside his bed he lay back on the bed and pulled the cord to extinguish the light above him. His head-ache still persisted but the darkness somehow seemed to soothe his mind.

The delectable smell of Angie lingered on the pillow next to him and had a calming effect. He began to analyse himself and his actions. Tonight he'd fully intended to cause some damage to Goulder's car, putting it out of action, and he realised that he saw the car as a symbol of attraction for Angie. Now he could see the futility of his intentions and the danger that he was putting himself into. This damned jealousy was leading him into a dangerous depression. His eyes filled with tears and he buried his face into the pillow. Why couldn't he be more like everyone else?, he asked himself. Why couldn't he just accept that Angie was a beautiful woman who was bound to be attractive to other men and just be thankful that she only had eyes for him?

His mind went back to this evening – the evidence was clear enough. There was a meeting at the house! There was an upstairs window lit and that was probably Goulder's office and he probably did remain there throughout!

He'd just resolved in his mind to fight this silly depression and this unreasonable jealousy when Angie entered the bedroom and switched on the lights. Mike shielded his eyes against the brightness but he wasn't quick enough.

"Mike, what's the matter you look as though you've been crying?"
She sat down on the bed beside him.

"No, it's just the bright light that makes my eyes water." Angie took his head in her arms and cradled him against her bosom.

"Michael, there's something wrong, I know it. Why can't you open up and tell me? Come on, whatever this is we can work it out together if you'll just tell me."

She held him close and ran her fingers gently through his hair. There was a silence for a moment and then Mike asked,

"Angie, you do still love me don't you?"

"Of course I do, surely you know I do; what's brought this on?"

Almost reluctantly Mike said,

"I began to think I was losing you."

"Oh, Mikey, Mikey, I know we've had some rough moments and perhaps I've not been as understanding as I could have been, but there's never been a moment when I've stopped loving you."

"You're not having an affair are you. I wouldn't blame you if you were, but you would tell me wouldn't you?"

"Whatever's given you that idea?"

"I saw you in Goulder's car the other night."

"Oh Mikey, Mikey. I thought there was trust between us. It upsets me that you'd think such a thing. Yes, I was in his car – Janice borrowed it to save shuffling about to get her's out. She was running me back to pick up my car from the railway station. I'd met her off the train earlier, and she wanted me to go with her to the warehouse to take some boxes. It seemed stupid to take two cars when she had hers so I went with her. That meant when we'd finished I had to get back to pick up my mini."

Mike wrapped his arms around her and his eyes filled again. They sank back onto the bed and lay entwined. It felt as though a huge weight had been taken off his shoulders. Nothing more was said.

At breakfast there was still more affection between the two than had been for some considerable time, and Mike left for work with a kiss.

"God, I feel better...." he remarked to himself as he got into his car, "...I've got to work at this; alter my attitude", as he reversed into the road.

The journey to work seemed to fly by and he realised his tolerance to other car drivers was also better – but wasn't to last.. He parked his car in the secure car park and made his way through the public foyer of the police station, pausing at the internal door where he began to punch the security number into the lock system. Suddenly, a voice shouted from behind him,

"Hey, Borman, wait a minute".
He looked behind him to see a uniform inspector sprinting across the foyer towards him. Before the inspector could say anything more, the habit of a life-time's aggression took over in Mike and he said, brusquely,

"I don't respond to 'Hey' from anyone and furthermore, my name has got a handle in front of it. I'm either Mister Borman or Sergeant. Take your choice, but I deserve as much respect from you as anyone else."
The inspector was clearly taken aback.

"I'm sorry sergeant..." he began, "...I didn't mean to offend you, you see I'm ex-forces and it's perfectly normal to address someone just by their surname. If it upsets you I won't do it again. It's just that I've had a message through from Inspector Allen from 'C' Division for you to the effect that they've identified the Rover car and interviewed the registered owner but it appears that he sold the car to someone whose identity he doesn't know. They've obtained a statement that will be forwarded to you and the man has been reported for failing to notify change of ownership. That's the message."

Mike realised he'd slipped off his pedestal after vowing to change his attitude and somewhat sheepishly he said to the inspector,

"Thanks. Look, I'm sorry I just went off the deep end. I know it's a lame excuse but I've had a heavy few days recently and

I've been feeling the pressure. My name's Mike", and he extended his hand towards the inspector.

"That's O.K..." he replied, taking Mike's hand in a very firm grip, "...Mike, we all have our moments. My name's Pete – Pete Byrne. I'm in Comms – if you want anything, I'm your man", he hand said with a smile that showed no hurt feelings.

. Mike went on his way towards his office feeling a bit better in himself for having apologised. He vowed to himself that he wouldn't let it happen again.

Chapter 7

Undercover

As Mike sat at his desk studying the night-log, David Scott appeared and sat on the corner of the desk.

"Mike, the Met chaps from the Anti- Terrorism Squad, are in with the Gov'nor. He wants us to join them in his office."
Andy Parr joined them and they walked the short distance along the corridor where they paused to press the button at the door to Detective Superintendent Birchall's office. The green 'Enter' light came on and Mike opened the door giving a single rap with his knuckle as they entered.

The hum of conversation between the occupants of the room suddenly stopped and Alan Birchall stood to greet the newcomers introducing them to the gathering.

"You've already met my Detective Inspector, Jimmy Johnson (and Birchall extended his hand to indicate Jimmy sitting in the corner with a pencil to his mouth seemingly like a placebo for his prohibited cigarettes). This is (indicating each in turn) my Detective Sergeant, Mike Borman, Dc.David Scott, and Dc.Andy Parr, and together we've been handling the enquiry so far."

A tall, young, dark haired officer in a smartly cut, blue, pin striped suit stepped forward, and introduced himself as Detective Superintendent John Churchill.

Mike didn't murmur but the thought went through his mind that Churchill was probably younger than him and he couldn't help but think in jealous terms how such a young individual had achieved such rank whilst he was languishing in the rank of Detective Sergeant. Churchill's appearance wouldn't have put him out of place at a high powered city executive business meeting.

"This is my Detective Chief Inspector Terry Jones..." (he was at least eight or ten years older than his boss) "...this is Detective Sergeant Will Smith (a mere boy - obviously on the 'fast track' system). and hopefully, we'll be joined by another officer later this morning. He's a specially trained officer of

Asian origin who will work undercover." He looked around to ensure he had everyone's attention before continuing.

"I want you to meet him but – and this I want to emphasize this – he'll not normally visit this police station or identify himself as a police officer and no-one must acknowledge him in public. He will be just another Islamic 'Joe Public' as far as we're concerned, and he'll report only to me."

Mike took his cue from Birchall and filled the kettle, and whilst it began to sing he took out eight mugs from a cupboard beneath the table. His voice carried across the room,

"Who wants tea, and who wants coffee?" and the response brought most of them crowding around Mike's cafeteria.

The following hour was taken up with Birchall and Mike leading the gathering in a disclosure and dissemination of the facts of the incident so far, the enquiries already put in place and the results. There was no criticism only slight disappointment that the press had already got hold of the fact that there was something big afoot. Appreciation was shown in that Mike had at least contained press disclosure for the moment.

An adjournment was called for and Birchall suggested the nearby Celandine Restaurant for an 'expenses' lunch where they could get to know each other in a more informal way.

The place was 'licensed' and those that wanted a drink with their lunch could avail themselves. The management were used to occasional police lunches and knew well enough the discretion required and usually a private function room would be provided, away from the public ear. A relaxed and satisfying sojourn filled part of the afternoon but they were eager to discuss the matter in hand throughout.

Accommodation in the police headquarters was always difficult to arrange; there was never enough rooms to suit their needs as specialist groups were forever being created. However, the needs of this anti-terrorist squad were paramount. The room had to be secure with secure telephone lines and computer access which couldn't be set up in an instant and the only option had to be within the existing Special Branch suite that was already equipped with all the facilities.

Birchall thought hard about the matter and came to the conclusion that the only option was for him to vacate his own office and move in with Jimmy.

"I know there's not a lot of room, Jimmy, but we'll have to manage – and before we go any further we'll have no smoking in the room, please. Empty the ash-tray and get some air-freshener sprayed around."

"Dammit Alan, I can't work all day without a fag."

"You'll just have to go outside for a smoke. I'm not breathing your second-hand smoke all day."
It was all light hearted but truly meant. Two more desks were quickly found and extra computer terminals established.

It was very soon apparent where Will Smith's expertise lay as he took over the computer to establish the encrypted links with the Met's Special Branch records. Mike found himself detailed to partner Chief Inspector Jones – Terry, and familiarise him with Crenarth and the areas of special interest. First the site of the burned out car and the body, second the Wheatsheaf public house where Dr. Rajavi had the encounter with the suspects, then the University and finally a general tour of the city taking in the central mosque. Mike found conversation with this genial Welshman very easy, there was no superior edge to him and the lilt of that accent he found quite endearing.

Terry produced his wallet and withdrew a photograph. It was becoming a little creased and dog-eared on the corners, but never-the-less was a lovely photograph of his wife, Gwynneth, and their two small girls. He was obviously very proud of his family.

"It was taken a few years ago in Cardiff, before I transferred to the Met. The girls are eight and ten now", he explained.

"I've only got the photo on my desk in the office - it's my wife Angie. We don't have any kids yet", said Mike.

"Do you both work, Mike?"

"Well, yes, I suppose so. Angie didn't work until recently but she's just got her foot in the door at a television company making commercials and that sort of stuff. We don't know where it'll lead yet."

After a short lull in the conversation Mike said,

"When you've got a bit of spare time I'll show you where I live and introduce you to Angie. She's bound to be interested in your wife and kids."

"That'll be nice. It's good to get to know someone personally when you're out on these jobs. It's not always easy – there's rarely the time."

Arriving back at Crenarth headquarters they made their way to the conference that had been called. One by one the full complement of the Special Branch office arrived at their desks and their numbers were swelled by the three Met officers who had with them a rough looking individual, quite young and clearly Arabic in appearance. The newcomer noticed Mike's astonishment and in a moment of mischievousness, placed his hand to his forehead, bowed his head and said "Salaam". Mike hardly knew what response to give but before he could speak the prankster said,

"Detective Sergeant Saied Asghar, Ayatollah to the Metropolitan Constabulary", and he extended his hand to Mike with a broad grin across his face. There was laughter across the room as Mike took his hand in a firm grip and responded,

"Good to meet you, I'm Mike. Sorry, I didn't catch your name properly."

Saied replied, "Yes, I know who you are, I'm fairly well briefed – just call me Sie, everybody else does."

Alan Birchall, spoke up from the rear of the gathering,

"Now we've all met, I want you all to settle, just find a chair and we'll begin." There was a shuffling of chairs as everyone found a seat and Birchall waited for quiet to descend and then continued,

"I'll get Detective Sergeant Borman to kick off by going over the details of everything that's happened so far and what enquiries have already been put in place especially for the benefit of Detective Sergeant Asghar. Mike, over to you."

Mike stood and faced the gathering and then went over the whole story again – from the meeting of Doctor Ali with the men enquiring about explosive chemicals, through the finding of the burned out car and the body, the forensic examination, the post mortem examination, and then step by step detailed the enquiries and results that had been made.

Detective Superintendent Churchill rose from his chair and stepped to the front. Leaning on the desk he began,

"You all know who I am, I'm Detective Superintendent John Churchill – John to all of you. You've already met my squad and our brilliant undercover man, Detective Sergeant Saied Asghar here; Sie as he's affectionately known. Now, Sorry to repeat myself but I must make this clear to you, this is the one and only time you'll have contact with Sie. It's important that you meet him so that you recognise him and don't compromise him at any time – to all intents and purposes you'll act as though you've never met him before and don't know him. He'll never come near this police station again – he's been ushered in by the back door so that he couldn't be observed by anyone other than us. I'm his contact and he'll keep in touch daily. Remember, his position could be extremely dangerous if his true identity should become known. I'm going to ask Sie to give us all a thumbnail picture of who we're probably dealing with."

Sie pushed his way to the front and confidently sat on the front desk. He began,

"We've all had a belly full of terrorism in this country but it's not just confined to this country, it's world-wide. We seem to have plenty of disaffected people who find reason to use violence to disrupt our lives.

"Look, I can sit here and bore you to death with a history of what's led to where we stand today with terrorism but it isn't going to help you to identify those we're looking for. I've seen it all and I'm fortunate in that I'm probably better placed than any of you to get information, just by moving in the asian community. You know, or maybe you don't, the majority of asian people are good people but because of their experience of the police in their own countries, they are very wary of you. They will talk to me as long as they don't suspect that I'm a police officer. That's why I don't want anyone to acknowledge me. Just walk by as though you've never seen me." Sie stood up looked around.

"I just want to say that my governor, John Churchill here, is in touch with me most of the time. He'll help you with anything and he can pass messages on to me if you want to warn me of anything or wish me to make enquiries in any particular direction. Thanks for having me here, I'll leave you in the hands of John Churchill. Good hunting."

Churchill spoke again, "As you'd expect, the Metropolitan Counter Terrorism organisation keeps a very close weather eye upon all those entering these shores through our immigration controls, also noting those people who travel to those areas of the middle east that seem to engender trouble. We also check through our registries which throw people of interest at times..There are two other things that Will Smith has at his disposal – which I would ask you to keep very quite about –one is the scanning of e-mail content by electronic monitor that focuses on key words, and the other, a similar monitoring of the air-waves - mobile 'phones and land lines - by GCHQ."

Detective Superintendent Birchall stood and thanked Sie and Mr Churchill for their contribution and then addressing his own officers said,

"You've all seen Sie now and I trust you're all experienced and sensible enough to understand that to recognise him and speak to him is enough to expose him and ruin this operation. O.K everyone lets get started – remember - everything, every snippet of information regardless of how small, goes through Will Smith in the office here. He'll oversee the dissemination of all the enquiry throws up and with our own typists will send out the actions each day."

As Mike collected the empty mugs and people rose to leave the office, Aland Birchill caught everyone's attention to say,

"Mr. Churchill here will be the supervising officer and will take all the executive decisions together with me. If there's anything contentious then ask either of us about it. The ACC's Incident Room and murder enquiry will be conducted separately by the uniform and CID sections to cover all the extranious stuff but everything they do will be filtered by us." He continued,

......"That allows us to concentrate on the subversive and terrorist aspects. OK folks, this is the fourth day since the body was found and it seems to me the clock is ticking. There's only going to be so much time before these idiots do their worst. It's up to us now. Let's get to it and stop them before they're able to cause their mayhem."

Before anyone could leave David Scott rapped loudly on the table to draw attention to himself.

"I've just received a telephone call with information that there's a protest march afoot. I've got no confirmation of this yet but it's come from the university and if the information is correct there's high feeling amongst the Asian students about the level of police interference. That might well be down to the uniform branch paying particular attention to them on our behalf. I'll dig a little deeper and try to find out more".

"O.K David, thanks for that. Keep us informed and be sure to make your report to Will Smith here – and that goes for everyone, anything, even the slightest bit of information, must be reported to the Detective Sergeant", added Birchall.

At the University Mustafa Osman, a 22 years old medical student in his third year, was discreetly engaged in a telephone conversation with David Scott, confirming that the Students' Union were organising a public protest against the inhuman and racist tactics of the Crenarth police. The 'Stop and Search' measures that were being employed they saw as being far beyond the legal powers of the police and were clearly an intimidation.

Mustafa had been David Scott's 'covert' for eighteen months and had received a monthly emolument that ultimately came from the treasury through the Security Service and the Special Branch and was a payment that the tax man would never know about. For this small but very welcome amount Mustafa was required to maintain his position of treasurer within the Students' Union and report any activities that might be required of him. A further requirement within the past eighteen months had been to join the Communist Party within the University and report on members and activities.

"I've just come from a union meeting and there's been some arguing about what's going to happen. There's some dissent because they're protesting against the police and the majority felt we shouldn't warn them that it was going to happen but we've got law students on the committee and they've insisted that to march through the streets to the police headquarters we're legally bound to give the police six days clear notice. Apparently it's covered by some Public Order Act. Anyway, the motion to comply was carried and it's arranged for Saturday, the 15th at eleven, and they're going to march through the town centre, past City Hall, and then double back past the Railway Station to the Police Headquarters where they're going to hand in a petition", reported Mustafa.

"O.K. Well, I know this is outside your usual remit but you must keep tabs on this and any other arrangements and let me know. I've told you what this is all about and you know how serious it is, so keep in touch and when this is all over there'll be something a little extra for you", said David, and the line went dead. He lost no time at all reporting in to Will Smith who responded,

"Great. Something seems to be working; let's just hope it's enough to make them show their hand. I'll arrange for video coverage and I'll call in all the CCTV footage. Thanks Dave."

Chapter 8

Psycology

Mike opened the door to be met by an excited Angie.

"I've got it Mike – I've got it….." she almost squealed, "…..I start Monday. Janice rang this afternoon. It's only a clerical job but I've got to start somewhere and she's as
good as promised to teach me everything about the business." She flung her arms around Mike and hugged him with a fervour as though she'd just won the lottery.

"That's great Ang I'm really pleased for you; truly", and for once he was being sincere. It was only then that she realised that someone was with Mike as he turned to invite Terry inside.

"Sorry about that Terry, Angie's been after a job with a small film and television company and as you heard she's got it", said Mike.

"Yes, I heard. Congratulations seem to be in order Mrs Borman."

"Sorry Angie, this is my friend Terry Jones. He's a Detective Chief Inspector up here from the Met. I've invited him round to meet you", explained Mike.

"That's nice. It's a pleasure to meet you Terry. If you hadn't already gathered, I'm Angie", and she thrust out her hand in a very warm gesture.

"Have you eaten?" Angie asked the two of them.

"No. I was hoping you might rustle up something – either that or I'll nip to the take-away?" said Mike.

"No, if you'll just bear with me I'll fix something – it won't be anything elaborate. Have you any objection to chicken in white sauce, Terry? It'll be from a tin but I can soon boil up some rice", asked Angie.

"That'll be fine, thank you. I've brought a bottle of plonk with me, perhaps you'll share that?"

As Mike and Terry settled in the lounge Angie retired to the kitchen to prepare the meal. She had to raise her voice to carry on a conversation.

"I don't know what it's like for you, Terry, but Mike's been keeping such dreadful hours; I never know when he's coming home. It's so bad I can't cook a meal for any particular time. He's so used to coming home to a cold dinner – thank goodness for micro waves."

"Oh, it's no different. I think it must be the same for every detective. It's probably worse for my wife. I get sent all over the country at a moment's notice and to be quite truthful it gets to be quite a strain on her."

"You are married then?" asked Angie.

"Yes, a lovely girl, Gwynneth, from back in Cardiff and we've two wonderful children, both girls. Megan eight and Rhiannan ten. Gwynneth jokes that she keeps a photograph of me on the mantelpiece so the children recognise me when I walk through the door. She is joking but deep down there's an element of reality and frustration there." He reached for his wallet and took out the photograph of his family.

"I've a photograph of them here. I'll show you when join us."

"How long have you been in the force, Terry?" asked Mike as he laid the table.

"I've been with the Met fourteen years now but I spent four years at Cardiff before I transferred."

"I only asked because you seem to be the oldest of your squad – even older than your boss."

"Yes. I'm from the old school, I've worked my way up by sheer hard work and determination. Don't get me wrong though, John Churchill, and even Will Smith are very clever men with a university education and they were destined for high rank the minute they joined. I wouldn't mind hazarding a guess that John Churchill will end up Commissioner one day – and I'd go further and say it won't be long."

Angie appeared from the kitchen carrying three plates with the expertise of a waiter and called both men to the table. Mike uncorked the wine and poured. Angie picked up Terry's photograph,

"Oh Terry, they're beautiful, you must be so proud."

"Yes, I am" and he raised his glass and said, "Here's to family" and all three clinked glasses and sipped. As they ate Terry continued the conversation,

"How long have you been in this job, Mike?"

"I've been in the force twelve years but I've only been in the S.B these last four.", he replied.

"What's holding you back?"

Mike looked somewhat bemused by the question but Angie jumped in with both feet,

"I'll tell you what's holding him back, it's his attitude. He likes to think he's his own man and he's got little or no patience with some others."

Mike put down his knife and fork and looked sideways at Angie but he paused before he spoke.

"I suppose Angie's right – to a degree, but I've been doing a bit of self analysis lately and I think my 'attitude' to which Angie refers, is tempered by several things." He hesitated again and said,

"Hey Terry, you didn't come here tonight to listen to this sort of thing," but Terry insisted,

"Come on, let's hear it. I asked you – it isn't as though you're foisting it on me".

"O.K. well, it's a bit introspective but here goes. I think it's all come about with this 'fast track' business, where they're recruiting university graduates and giving them guarantees of quick promotion. Don't get me wrong, there are some that are worthy of their promotions, but there seem to be a lot more who are academically very clever but severely lacking in common sense".

He took a moment to gather his thoughts. He didn't want to sound like some pathetic idiot. After a deep breath he continued,

"I've had some poor experiences with them and the one thing that a copper needs, whether he's a uniform constable or higher rank, is common sense."

This really was self analysis. He continued,

......"The other thing is 'man management' because half the time the attitude of some – not all – to others lacks fundamental courtesy. That's where Angie sees my 'attitude' as being aggressive whereas I see it as standing up for myself and demanding the same courtesy as they would expect."

"But Mikey darling, don't you see that you'd be better thought of if you just let it wash over you – just as though it didn't affect you?"

"I can't do that. If someone, even a senior officer, says something to me that I regard as offensive – or basically wrong – I can't let it pass."
Mike drained his glass and looked up at Terry,

"Come on, let's leave it – this is getting like a psychoanalyst's group meeting."

"Well, it's interesting because that's one of my jobs when our Squad becomes engaged in any enquiry. A small part of my job is to assess the people we're working with. Don't worry Mike, I made my mind up about you very early on in our meeting."

"Are you some sort of psychiatrist then?" asked Angie.

"Psychologist, Angie. Psychologist is what you mean", corrected Mike.
Terry took no heed and replied,

"No, not at all. But we're taught to weigh up who we're working with because we need to know who we can depend upon in a tight corner. It sounds a bit melodramatic and we have to be careful not to offend anyone".

"Well, what did you make of me?" asked Mike.

"I think it speaks for itself that I'm here with you tonight. I found you a very personable detective who believes strongly in the job you're doing. Plenty of commitment and lots of ability. It's because you've plenty of ability that made me ask what was holding you back. There's got to be something – or someone."
Terry looked questioningly at Mike, then said,

"You've plenty of commendations on your personal record so you should be one of the front runners for promotion. If you really want promotion you've got to assess what it is that's holding you back, and change it – even if it hurts your pride. Now, if it's someone above you that's taken a dislike to you and he's the culprit then I would suggest a transfer. That's exactly why I transferred to the Met. It's well worth thinking about Mike, the Met's so big the opportunities are immense."

"Oh, I've thought about it, Terry, but you've got to admit it's difficult. When you're married you've both got to be agreeable to a move like that and I don't think it would suit Angie", said Mike and he looked to Angie to hear her response.

"No, not just at this moment, I don't think I'd want to move; especially having just got this opportunity with Janice."

"You're correct; both of you have got to be of the same mind. It all boils down to the question, 'How ambitious are you and are you both of the same mind?'

"If you've both finished let's clear away and sit in a bit more comfort", said Angie and she rose, gathered the plates, and took them to the kitchen. She returned with another bottle of wine; this time a Spanish Sauterne which was more to her taste. Mike took the bottle and uncorked whilst Angie produced fresh glasses.

Chapter 9

The Protest March

Tariq Jamil, with his ideas of film in mind, had identified a group within the mosque who displayed a sense of disenchantment, with both the Imam and the elders. Since the adhan (the call to prayer) by the Muezzin, Tariq had waited around the wash-room dragging out his 'Taharah' (the ritual washing) waiting to catch sight of one or more of the group of young men he'd become interested in, before entering the temple.

He took up a position alongside them and rolled out his prayer mat in preparation for his Salat (the prayer ritual). He raised his hands to head level and uttered the takbir (Allah Akbar – God is great) aloud. With his hands at his side he pronounced the first sura (a passage of the Qur'an) then another takbir. With his hands on his knees he bowed forwards saying "Glory to God the Almighty."

Standing upright again he said, "God hears those who praise Him. Oh our Lord, praise be to You", and then another takbir. Kneeling, he bent his body forward until his forehead touched the floor in the usual supplication, with hands flat on the floor. ......Sitting back on his heels he lifted his hands with palms uppermost mumbling an almost silent prayer, "Praise be to my Lord most high; praise be to Him", and then repeated the supplication and the prayer three times. Finally another takbir - "Allah Akbar."

As the devotions of the salat (this five times daily formal prayer ritual) ended and the faithful began to leave, he quickly recovered his shoes and hastily slipped them on as he rushed to catch up with the group of young men. His daily prayers and his bonhomie had served him well amongst those whom he sought to befriend but this small group of four were more difficult to penetrate.

There seemed something about these four that stood them apart. Their devotions were sincere but their general attitude was rather surly and remote. Tariq was working hard to engender some sort of relationship with them but he wasn't accepted. He sensed that they regarded him with suspicion. He came abreast of them on the outside of the pavement and they turned to look at him with a manner that shouted "Get lost".

"Salam alaikum. Have you heard about the protest march?" he asked them.

"What protest march?"

"It's the students at the university. They're protesting against the continual 'stop and search' campaign by the police against the Asian students. They're going to march through the city centre to the police headquarters", Tariq said as he looked for some response. The nearest of the four, who appeared to be the youngest, turned to Tariq with a smirk and said,

"March, what good will that do? There'll be a far bigger protest in-sha'Allah (God willing)......", but before he could finish his sentence one of the older men grabbed him by the shirt front in an angry display, obviously to silence him.

Tariq made no remark on the incident but continued to walk with them for some short distance before he made his excuse and parted company in a different direction.

There was no fond farewell. His mind raced, sure that he had stumbled upon the element likely to lead him to a likely story for his program. What did he mean, 'There'll be a far bigger protest…', and if there was nothing to it then why did they grab hold of him to shut him up?

He felt excited. He'd identified them now he needed to work on them, to find out who they were, what they were, and try get their confidence.

Detective Sergeant Saied Asghar clicked away with his camera, his telephoto lens bringing them into full screen. When Tariq and the five split to go their separate ways Sie had to make a decision and he chose to follow the four. They entered the municipal park and sat on the steps of the bandstand. He observed that there was some altercation between them that seemed to be directed at the youngest. His camera continued to click away.

That same afternoon D/Superintendent Churchill downloaded Sie's memory card from the camera and printed off the photographs. There was a buzz around the office as everyone perused the photographs. None were readily identified but something at the back of Mike's mind told him he'd seen the Omar Sharif look-alike with the silvering hair before, but try as he might he couldn't bring him to mind.

"Andy take these copies and show them to doctor Rajavi. See if he can identify any of them....", said Mike, "....there's always the chance one of them could be one of the guys who approached him."

Turning to David Scott he said,

"David, get these blown up – A4 size – and take them down to the uniform section and get them to pin them up on the notice board so that every beat officer sees them but make sure that they're instructed that no-one should approach them. Identification is all that's needed."

Sie returned to the mosque. Mohammed Aaymer, the Imam, was a doctor of philosophy, and as Mufti was a wise moderate in his interpretation of Shari'a Law. He was nearing the end of his tenure of imamate. Sie had quickly fostered a relationship without divulging his purpose or his status. He subtly probed to gain some identification of the five but his oblique questions only revealed general information.

Perhaps, he thought, the Imam was just as crafty as himself because it seemed that without direct questions each enquiry was answered in a very non-specific manner. However, he did learn that the five had been exceptionally vocal in their opposition to the American obscenity of 'extraordinary rendition' where they secretly removed prisoners to their bases in countries where, it was widely considered they could torture them with impunity, or at least without too much public outcry, to obtain confessions. Guantanamo Bay, the American detention camp on Cuba figured very largely in their discussions, but they were not exceptional in that.

What had been slightly alarming for the Imam was that they saw the government of Great Britain complicit in this detention, rendition and torture. Their rhetoric had been to align the government to that of Vichy France during the Second World War and their complicity in surrendering French citizens to the Nazi tyrants and ultimately to the gas chambers.

He'd neither seen nor heard anything that would lead him to believe that they had taken this matter beyond healthy discussion and believed most of their talk was just posturing against the peaceable and conciliatory faction of the elders. Never-the-less it was clear he felt slightly concerned about them. Sie left the Imam with his usual

"Al-hamdu li-Llah (hamdulah – Praise be to God)."

Andy Parr met Doctor Rajavi by arrangement and showed the photographs that Sie had taken.

"I can't be sure", he said but he lingered long over one photograph and studied it hard.

"This could be one of them – it's difficult to be sure. His face seems very familiar but am I remembering him from that meeting or perhaps from somewhere else?"

"I know it's difficult but do try to remember."

"I'm tempted to say yes, he's one of them, but I'm not absolutely sure. I've spent a long time at the university trying to find some face or name that I recognise but, without taking the clerical staff into my confidence I couldn't manage anything. I wasn't about to tell just anyone about this. My problem is that as an outside lecturer I don't have access to student details."

"That's understandable..." said Andy, "... but we have obtained those lists of students who were studying chemistry and may have attended your lectures and we'll go through them with you. You may pick someone out from that."

"Have you heard that there's some sort of student protest march being planned?" asked the doctor.

"Yes, we've heard. It's some protest about the 'stop and search' tactics being used by the uniform branch. We initiated those tactics simply to get some idea of the numbers and the feelings of students. I believe the thinking behind it was that there may have been some useful contact made that would give us a lead."

"Forgive me, I don't want to tell you how to do your job, but I fear that's the wrong way to go about it. You're treading a very fine line in dealing with these youngsters. It's a line between acceptance and incitement. I don't suppose you saw it but there was a Channel Four television program recently that was all about Muslim opinion." He pushed the photographs away across the table before continuing, "...I think it was as a result of a National Opinion Poll. It was very depressing viewing. It concluded that the Muslim threat to security in the UK was so severe that the Assistant Commissioner for Police in London, Tarique Ghaffur has called for an inquiry into the radicalization of young Muslims. He described them as 'a generation of angry young people vulnerable to exploitation." Andy could only nod his head in agreement. Doctor Rajavi wasn't finished,

"It's frightening to think that these are the very people that extremists prey upon. I know from my own experience that these young men are already alienated and   susceptible to the radical views of extremists. If I could offer a small token of advice it would be to handle them with a little more respect – a little more gently. I don't think that such confrontational measures as the 'stop and Search' will work."

Andy smiled and extended his palms in a gesture of resignation,

"I understand what you say but unfortunately I don't dictate policy or strategy."

"No, I know, and what I've just said is meant to be helpful. Perhaps you might just influence your superiors a little if you mention our conversation."

"I'll mention it but whether they listen is quite another matter. Before I go can I enquire what exactly did you mean when you said that from your own experience these young Muslims were alienated and susceptible?"

"It's a matter of general knowledge that there's a great deal of money and influence coming from the Saudis at the moment. Their radicalism is the insidious problem that exists and is growing. That's one of the main reasons for the alienation of the young. We're very fortunate here to have Dr. Aaymer as the imam. He's what you'd describe as a moderate, but there are quite a number of imams about the country, especially in the capital, who are of the old school and are extremely influenced by this Saudi Wahhibi doctrine. If you've got such firebrands

indoctrinating the young then you can but expect extremism from them and there's nothing the Saudis would like better than to see this radicalism undermine the UK. I'm sorry, I perhaps show too much passion, but I strongly believe that that's where our problems lie."
The two men stood and shook hands before parting.

Chapter 10

Journalism and the promise.

Guy Palmer, the reporter, sat patiently waiting in the foyer of the police headquarters, determined to follow up on his story. He felt as though he was getting the 'brush off' big time from everyone. He'd been there for more than half an hour, just twiddling his thumbs, waiting for Mike Borman and there seemed no response. He rose from his seat again and pressed the inset bell in the enquiry desk counter. A young female office clerk came to the window.

He was about to voice his frustration to her when Mike suddenly appeared from a side door. He turned to Mike leaving the office clerk somewhat bewildered.

"Mike, I've had nothing from you about this body. What's happening? I can't sit on it for ever and it's six days now."

"Well, I was hoping to hear from you. I saw your little piece in the paper asking for help in identifying the body but I expected you to let us know about the response."

"The plain fact is there's been no response. Oh, we've had the usual nutters ringing up, a so called clairvoyant, and an obvious weirdo but nothing positive."

"O.K. Well, I'd appreciate knowing who these nutters, the weirdoes and the clairvoyant are – you see we still need to check them out. I can't divulge much more about the body until I've spoken to my boss. Just a hint – we're actually looking towards the Asian community. Keep a lid on it and I promise you, you'll get the whole story when it breaks – I think it will be big."

Palmer's mind went into overdrive and his face and eyes contracted into a quizzical expression,

"Hey, this is something to do with terrorism isn't it? Come on Mike, level with me. I've got a nose for a story – I'm right aren't I?"

"Look, we don't know what the devil we're dealing with yet. The reason we've kept a lid on it so far is because we don't want to frighten people and we don't want to give the game away to who-ever else is involved. I'm trusting you, Guy, to keep your word. Don't print anything that's going to blow it for us and I promise as soon as I can I'll give you the scoop."

"That's OK but you've got to understand that I've got an editor to account to. I'll do my best but I'm under pressure to get a story so the sooner you can let me have something the easier it'll be for me."

They shook hands and Palmer left. Mike returned upstairs to the Special Branch office complex. Alan Birchall was out for some reason but D/Superintendent Churchill was going through some of the latest paper work returned by the squad.

"Can I see you for a minute, Sir?"

"John – it's John to you."

"Thank's Sir, er John, We've got a bit of a problem brewing. As you know, a local reporter from the Crenarth Post and Times, picked up on the body in the burned out car. We, that is I, made an agreement with him to just run a piece in the paper saying that the body had been found but purely asking for assistance from the readers in identifying the body. In return I've promised him the exclusive when we're in a position to release the information."

"Yes, I know all about that."

"Well, he's turned up here today trying to get something on the story. I've tried to keep him happy but I think he's sussed out what it's all about. He's gone away giving me his assurance that he won't blow the gaff but frankly I'm a bit concerned."

"I see. Leave it with me. I'll have words with his editor. I can bring pressure to bear and I'm sure he'll listen to me. I'll give him the same promise – that he can have the scoop. As you're probably aware, if it came to it I could get the Home Secretary to issue a 'D' notice preventing the newspaper printing anything - but to do that would alert all the major papers and agencies and we'd certainly have the whole lot of them up here under our feet. I think it's much better to deal with this on a personal basis."

The days slipped by without much progress in the enquiry and in the morning of the tenth day the students began to gather around the steps of the university. By eleven o'clock about seventy or eighty had joined the throng, and they seemed to be of all nationalities.

There seemed to be no organised leadership until four students arrived carrying arms full of placards. There was a surge to obtain one each but there were far too few to go round. They were very basic, constructed of a short wooden pole with a piece of hardboard nailed to the top. Each had been roughly painted white with a slogan in large black letters. "POLICE BRUTALITY", "NAZI POLICE" and even "RACIST PIGS" were easily identified amongst the placards.

More students joined the throng and they fell in behind two who stood out obvious organisers, who stretched a white banner between them which proclaimed, "POLICE RACIST TACTICS", which possibly had more relevance to their actual complaint.

As the procession set off filling the roadway, traffic which had avoided the police diversions was forced to a stop. The shouting and chanting seemed to grow ever louder as more people joined them. Police video cameras covered the beginning of the demonstration with the operators using the 'close up' facilities of the lenses to make identification of the participants easier. Mike, Andy and David, followed the procession and then skipping ahead to vantage points with their stills cameras, took copious photographs.

A three man crew with film camera and sound recording equipment also covered the scene. They had none of the usual emblems of recognisable TV companies such as BBC, ITV or SKY News. The third man of the crew was an Omar Sharif look-alike but he was muffled up against the cold and it was unlikely that he'd be recognised.

All the CCTV cameras were trained upon the route in anticipation. Police uniformed officers led the march and others performed traffic control duties at junctions but it was altogether a very low-key presence. Behind the scenes about a hundred officers drawn from all divisions of the city were held in reserve should riotous behaviour become apparent, and they sat around in the canteen, bored and annoyed at the waste of their time.

Those men trained in the control of public disorder, popularly referred to as the riot squad, dressed in their familiar protective clothing, helmets and shields, lounged in their vans in back streets within quick proximity of the protest route. Card games for petty stakes kept them occupied.

Assistant Chief Constable Michael Coverly together with several Chief Superintendents and Detective Superintendents John Churchill and Alan Birchall gathered in the force Operations Room where there was CCTV surveillance and wireless communication to all operational vehicles.

The personal wireless communications to individual officers was operated from divisional headquarters and those affected by this protest march would be contacted via Central Division.

The route from the university through the city centre to the City Hall took them past the railway station and then down Spring Gardens, the main shopping street. It was quite an orderly throng despite the banner and placard waving, the shouting and chanting.

The majority of shoppers took little notice of the clamour and, having looked at the approaching noisy marchers, turned away and carried on with their shopping. It appeared that it was – in modern parlance – a non-event, with little sympathy being given to their complaints by the local populace. The most response that seemed to be achieved was shouts of "disgraceful" at the placard carriers.

As the protest entered 'Curry Street' as the locals called it, actually Water Street, the occupants of the numerous restaurants did pay them more attention and actually left whatever they were doing to stand on the pavements and cheer the students, clearly showing some sort of Asian solidarity.

Outside the Taj Mahal Indian restaurant, Mike was interested in the tall young figure in the kitchen whites and the white cap who shouted encouragement in his native tongue. His bearded features seemed vaguely familiar. Mike steadied his camera and focused on the man's face filling the whole frame and took a series of photographs in quick succession.

The figure posed him quite a problem. He was sure he'd seen those features before, but where? He remained at his vantage point watching the protestors slowly pass but still kept his vigil upon the mystery man. He was satisfied when the man disappeared inside the Taj Mahal.

The protest worked its way along the main pedestrianised thoroughfare of Market Square until they reached City Hall where they bunched together in a ragged semi-circle before the marble steps. The local populace seemed to ignore the chanting, placard waving students dismissive of their complaints, much as had been the reaction along the route.

There was a definite presence of police uniforms around City Hall, albeit a restrained attitude. The chanting continued until a figure from their midst appeared before them with a megaphone to address who-ever would listen – but no-one appeared from the council chambers to receive the address.

Never-the-less, the spokesman shouted into the megaphone addressing who-ever he thought might be inside the building. His shouting merely produced loud squelches and ear-splitting screeches from the megaphone and most of what was shouted was lost in the cacophony.

Guy Palmer stood to one side making copious notes whilst his partner was taking photographs for the next edition of the Crenarth Post and Times.

With no success at the City Hall the march continued for the last half mile, past the railway station and 'bus terminal, to the Crenarth City Police Headquarters. The banner held high at the fore and the chanting and placard waving reached a high crescendo to create their best impression. The gates to the yard, where the police vehicles were parked, were closed and guarded.

The largest noticeable police presence so far, was displayed as a barrier to prevent the protesters gaining access to the building. Dog handlers were deployed at strategic points, the uniform officers who had been held in readiness were now deployed both in the barrier and in the box formation that contained the protesters.

The armoured people-carriers with their contingent of riot squad officers in their protective clothing, were brought into close proximity but the men remained within the vehicles. It was simply a show of strength to deter any breach of the peace.

The noisy marchers had shown no desire for physical confrontation and once more they bunched up around their leaders facing the black marble frontage of the police headquarters. The noisy throng became a little more subdued until two of their number walked forward towards the entrance and were met half way by the Assistant Chief Constable Michael Coverly.

The jeering and slogan shouting increased as a thick dossier of complaints was thrust at the Chief Constable. Guy Palmer's photographer snapped away to the intense shouting and gesticulating from the students.

The Chief Constable turned on his heels and disappeared inside the building and suddenly the spectacle was over. The marchers began to dissipate, watched carefully by the police presence.

"Well, that was a total waste of time and police manpower", remarked Andy Parr to Mike.

"We'll see when we've examined all the CCTV footage. At least we got away without any violence – which quite frankly I did expect."

Chapter 11

Aliens Registration

Detective Sergeant Will Smith and Mike sat together pouring over the photo's that had been rushed through and the CCTV footage from the whole of the march. There was nothing, absolutely nothing that gave them the slightest indication of who their suspected terrorists might be. There were several of the local troublemakers identified who had latched on to the protest hoping for a chance to get involved in a fight, but nothing! Nothing, that is, until Mike came to the photo's he'd taken of the bearded kitchen hand standing outside the Taj Mahal restaurant.

"He rings a bell somewhere in my mind but for the life of me I don't know why."

"Well, let's run him through the system then. He may be in the Criminal Records Office registers or, maybe, in your own Aliens Registration records, even your Collator's intelligence system. I'll fax a photo to the CRO first and get them to do an emergency search, then we'll both have a go at the Aliens Registration."

"He might be nothing to do with our enquiry, he might just be someone I've seen in the past."

"It doesn't matter, we've nothing else to go on and if it turns out to be useless, well, we've lost nothing, have we?"

Whilst he prepared the faxed request and the photograph for the Criminal Records Office Will made some serious observations about the government's policies on immigration and border controls since we joined the EEC.

"I'd better be careful what I'm saying, everybody's so damned politically correct these days but I can't help myself. The damned government seem to be so timid, almost bending over backwards to encourage this multi-culturalism", he said looking pensively at Mike.

"Will, it's nice to know there's someone else who thinks like me!", Mike said as they made their way to the Special Branch administration office.

The clerical staff had long since left at the end of a tiresome day, so they spread themselves out on the desks with the long narrow drawers containing the Aliens index extracted from the cabinets. They were in alphabetical order but that was no help to them. It was a matter of searching each card and the attached paperwork to find a photographic match for Mike's mystery man, and there were hundreds.

"You know we might be batting on a very sticky wicket here, he could well be an illegal, somebody who arrived in the back of a lorry – there's plenty of 'em. We're in for a late night, Mike".

"They're all late nights in this job I just hope Angie understands".

"Who's Angie ?"

"My wife. These late hours have been getting to her a bit just lately."

"That's why I'm still single", answered Will.

Card by card the registry was checked. It was an element of the Special Branch office that still hadn't been fully committed to disc for the computer system as it was a continual flow of aliens into and out of Crenarth, and until such time that the system was finally put in place, and fully operative, the card registry was kept as a necessity.

"My eyes are beginning to get a little sore...", said Mike, "...Shall we leave it for tonight and carry on in the morning?"

"No, let's do a few more. If you're fed up you go home, I'll carry on – I've got no wife to rush home to."

"I'll stay a while longer, but we shalln't get through them all tonight."

Suddenly Mike yelled out, "Eureeeeka. Got him."
Will looked over his shoulder to see for himself the photograph and read the details.

"Ayman Mohammed Bakri, born July 15, 1981, Kabol, Afghanistan."

"What the devil does this mean, Will? – Tadzhik, and Farsi?"

"Tadzhik are a race of people, probably originally from Iran and they speak a dialect which resembles Farsi which is the official spoken language of Iran. Hey, this is interesting, look - he's from Kabol and he has relatives over the border in Pashawar and Islamabad in Pakistan." Will took the card and photograph to study it more closely, He continued,

It might mean nothing at all but I'm surprised this card isn't flagged because that's the area where all the trouble has been. The Taliban are the freedom fighters – our terrorists – in Afghanistan who are being nurtured around that area of Pakistan. He's well worth looking at."

Mike took the card back to read then excitedly exclaimed,

"Look, this is our lucky day. His visa expired nearly six months ago. There's nothing on here about any application for extended leave to stay and there's nothing about any work permit."

"Right, let's have him in. We'll arrange some uniform for tomorrow morning, and we'll go into the Taj Mahal on an immigration check. There's no need to mention anything about terrorism until we get him in here. I've got a good feeling about this one, Mike. He's from exactly the place where I'd expect this radicalism."

Mike stayed behind just long enough to arrange with the uniform inspector for sufficient personnel for an immigration check at the Taj Mahal the following morning.

He sped home in a state of euphoria. The hour was very late. The hall light was burning but the remainder of the house was in darkness – Angie was obviously in bed. He threw off his raincoat and jacket, leaving them in a heap on the hall stand, and kicked off his shoes, then bounded up the stairs. Angie had drifted off into a pleasant dream and awoke with a start. She pulled the cord of the reading lamp above her head and sat upright as Mike blundered into the bedroom releasing his tie and unbuttoning his shirt.

"Sorry to wake you Ange – I'm just a bit excited, that's all", he said as he sat down on the bed and began to remove his trousers.

"I thought you were drunk."

"No. Plain cold sober but excited as hell."

"I've not seen you like this for a long time – have we won the lottery or something?"

"No, but it's something nearly as good."

"Well, what the devil is it, have I got to guess?" she asked, puzzled and a little irritated.

"It'll mean nothing to you, but I think we might have crackled it."

"God, Mike it's like trying to get blood out of a stone. Cracked what?", she asked, sleepy irritation now beginning to get the better of her.

"Didn't you wonder what Terry Jones was doing up here from the Met ?"

"No. It never crossed my mind to ask. You, above all, know how secretive you all are. I just thought 'If he wants me to know he'll tell me', and I never gave it another thought."
Angie lay back on the pillow as Mike explained,

"Well, the fact is we've a squad up from the Met to help us with an enquiry that might be connected to terrorism."
Angie looked at him with a quizzical expression,

"Terrorism ? What, here in Crenarth ?"

"Promise me not to say anything to anyone else, but you remember a few nights back when they rang me about the body in the burnt out car? Well, that body was put there to destroy evidence. He was actually killed by an explosion and the forensics seem to prove he was in the act of creating his own home-made explosive when it went off prematurely – and he died. We still haven't identified him and we've been struggling to get anywhere but tonight I think I've got our first lead. I've identified someone from the photos I took this afternoon that looks to be our first positive lead."

He reached over and pulled the cord to extinguish the light, then pulled Angie to him in a close embrace and kissed her passionately. His hands began to caress and wander but Angie said in a tired voice,

"I'm tired Mike, let me get some sleep, I have to be up early."

Mike lay on his back, hands behind his head, staring into a dark void, unable to sleep, with his mind turning over the day's events and thinking 'Oh please, let him be the key to this.' Try as he might he couldn't recall where he'd seen Bakri before and there was still the slightest of doubt that kept pricking at his mind, reminding him that this could still all fall flat. His rest was uneasy but gradually tiredness overtook him and he fell to sleep.

Daylight broke about 6.30am and a shaft of sunlight forced its way between the curtains. Mike had found it difficult to sleep and had been awake – or so he thought – for a considerable time. He threw back the duvet and swung his legs out of bed. He examined the bedside clock to reassure himself of the time. He felt the drag of tiredness but still there was excitement and expectation for the morning to come. He quickly shaved whilst Angie stirred from her blissful slumbers and slipped on her dressing gown. She approached Mike from behind, slid her arms around his waist and kissed the nape of his neck.

"God, Angie, you shouldn't do that to me first thing in a morning. You put some very naughty ideas into my head when we've both got to get to work."

With a sly look upon his face he dropped his razor into the bowl and turned and pulled her close, pressing his lips hard upon hers and leaving shaving cream on her nose and chin. She giggled, pushed him away, turned and ran back to the bedroom, leaving him to finish his ablutions.

Mike dressed quickly and was downstairs first to boil the kettle and make the tea whilst Angie prettied herself and powdered her nose. It was something of an oddity for them both to be able to take breakfast together and he couldn't help but think how different things had become between them in the past fortnight. It wasn't a cooked breakfast, unless you could call a boiled egg such, but they sat together sharing those few fleeting moments before they each had to start their day.

Chapter 12

The Taj Mahal

As usual Mike was the first to arrive at the office and he fetched the master key to the office from the safe in the control room. He unlocked and disabled the alarm system. By the time that Alan Birchall arrived Mike had typed out a brief and had organised the
daily rota for sufficient men to carry out a spot immigration check on the Taj Mahal.

At 10am a convoy of three unmarked cars and one police vehicle containing uniformed officers, drew to a halt outside the restaurant. There was no screeching of tyres to herald their arrival, just a quiet, speedy and efficient entry and a containment of the building to prevent any 'runners'. There were no customers as the restaurant wouldn't normally be open to the public before noon.

Mike made straight for the small back office where the surprised manager, Rahul Patel, sat engrossed in till rolls and invoices. Mike flashed his warrant card as Patel rose to his feet somewhat alarmed.

"Immigration check. How many people are there on the premises?"
Patel thought for a moment and then answered,
"Six in addition to me".
"Have them all gather here with their passports and visas, please. My officers will then search the building for anyone who fails to present himself – do you understand?"

"Yes, Sir. I understand perfectly well", Patel answered in excellent English, and summoned a young kitchen assistant to bring all the employees to the office. Slowly the six presented themselves and Patel identified them one by one.

"Passports and papers?" demanded Mike, and Patel turned about to open the corner safe.

The men were all separated and seated, each at a table, to be interviewed in turn by a police officer. Mike spotted the

83

bearded Ayman Mohammed Bakri, and proceeded to interview him. Terry Jones joined him as Patel produced Bakri's passport and his Aliens Registration booklet.

Whilst Mike examined the passport, Terry opened up the green coloured Aliens Registration document. Nothing was said between them for a while.

Mike and Terry looked at each other and immediately understood the implication as Terry pointed to the Aliens Registration which clearly showed the police stamp. Mike opened the passport at the immigration stamp which showed the period of permitted stay had expired. Terry beckoned Patel, the manager, to the table and said,

"This man is clearly in breach of his permission to remain in this country. You are in effect employing an illegal".

"No. No, Sir", Patel responded, rubbing his hands together nervously, "I personally have sent to the Home Office, his application for extended stay. We are still awaiting their reply."

Mike and Terry rose from the table and conversed quietly with each other, out of earshot of Patel and Bakri.

"His claim to have sent in an application for leave to stay beyond his allotted time, may be genuine, but it's strange that he hasn't submitted his passport and Aliens Registration document to the Home Office together with the application. There's enough suspicion here for us to hold him. Do you agree?"

"I agree. Let's nick him, we don't want him doing a runner," answered Mike.

Bakri was led, protesting, to the waiting police car whilst the checking of the remaining employees went ahead. Nothing more was found in the check and it appeared that Patel was otherwise a careful and law abiding employer.

Bakri sat dejected and silent in the interview room of the custody suite. He'd been led through the imposing, and somewhat daunting, iron gates of that secure cell block, to stand before the custody sergeant's desk. The gates had clanged behind him in a deliberate manner to emphasize his hopeless condition. A methodical search of his body, the removal of shoe laces and belt – albeit to prevent suicides –

was another drastic assault on his senses, and now he sat alone, bewildered and afraid. The windowless room itself was repressive.

In the SB office on the second floor, Mike and Terry gathered with Detective Superintendent Alan Birchall, Det Inspr Jimmy Johnson, Det Supt John Churchill, and Det Sergt Will Smith. Mike was the first to speak,

"How are we going to approach this, Guv", addressing Birchall.

"Well, the first thing is, does he understand sufficient English for us to interrogate him without an interpreter?"

"He seems to understand everything so far".

"OK, we'll do a preliminary and see how we get on, then if we decide we need an interpreter we'll get one."
Looking at the registration card from the index he said,

"It looks as though he speaks Farsi, whatever that is, God only knows where we'll find an interpreter who speaks Farsi".

"That's no problem....", interjected Mike, "....At least I don't think it is. The chemist who started this ball rolling, Doctor Rajavi, he speaks Farsi by the sounds of things. Will tells me it's the spoken language of Iran".

"OK, well he's detained under the Aliens Registration Act, 1914, as amended by the Aliens Order of 1960, so the first thing we must do is contact the Home Office to find out whether there was a genuine application for an extension of leave to stay – Will, can you do that, please, straight away?", asked John Churchill.

"I'll get to it this minute."
Speaking directly to Mike, Churchill then said,

"Alan Birchall and I will take a crack at him first. We're going in to put the fear of God up him. Afterwards I want you to go in and play the 'good guy', you know, befriend him. By the way, Mike, has it come back to you yet where you recognised him from?"

"No, Sir, it hasn't. I've been racking my brains, trying to remember – but nothing."

"Right-Oh, well, you're all familiar with dealing with prisoners but can I just remind you to enter all details of visits and interviews on the charge sheet – I'm sure the custody sergeant won't let you forget, but we want no cock-ups with this", said Birchall.

An hour passed and the two senior officers emerged from the custody suite in sombre mood which wasn't lifted by Will Smith's news that he'd been in touch with the Home Office Immigration Control who confirmed that Bakri had indeed submitted an application, furthermore, there had been some sort of administrative delay in notification but the application had been granted.

"Well, we've come unstuck with this one – we shall have to let him go", said Birchall.

"Before we let him go, just let me see what I can make of him, Guv", suggested Mike.

"OK. Nothing ventured, nothing gained."

Mike entered the interview room carrying two cups of tea which he set down on the table and invited the dejected Bakri to take one.

"I've put you two sugars in that. That should lift your spirits a bit. You look a bit down in the mouth."

"Down in the mouth?"

"Yes, a bit low in spirit."

"They're going to send me back to Kabol. I have good job here and I have lady. I do no wrong. I try to be good citizen. Why do they send me back? Why?"

"What do they call you – your friends, what do they call you?"

"Mohammed."

"Well, Mohammed, why do you think they're going to send you back?"

"They call me terrorist. They say I have made bombs to kill and injure people. They are wrong. I am not terrorist."

"I've met you before, Mohammed, but I can't remember where."

"Here at Police Station."

"Here? When?"

"Nearly two weeks. I came here to ask about my brother. You were with a police in uniform near the door. You said to go to enquiry desk." That was enough to spark Mike's memory,

"Ah yes, I remember. Did you find out what you wanted to know?"

"No. It was busy. I left."

"Well, perhaps I can help you. What did you want to know?"

"It not matter now. I cause problem."

"Problem? Problem for who?"

"I cause problem for my brother."

"Why would it cause a problem for your brother? Is it something I can help you with?"

"I don't like to say. I cause trouble."

"Well, you were sufficiently concerned about your brother to come here on that day. Why should it be any different now?"

"He disappeared."

"What do you mean – disappeared?".

"He here one day then suddenly disappear."

"What would make him disappear. Is it possible he's gone to visit someone – friends or family?"

"No. There is nobody. He left passport at home – no suitcase, no clothes."

Mike's mind began to work over-time; a missing brother who had taken nothing with him – not even his passport. Was this the body in the burned out car?

"Look, Mohammed. I think I might be able to help you; let you stay in this country. Do you understand? I have some influence here over who stays and who is sent back, but if I help you, then you must help me, agreed?" said Mike craftily using the knowledge that the Home Office had already granted the application.

"I stay if I help you?"

"Yes. I want you to tell me all about your brother and his friends."

"My brother is young man. Foolish young man. He does not listen to me. I try to keep him out of trouble. His friends are, how do you say – big problem. I do not like them; I think they cause big trouble."

"Why do they cause big trouble?"

"They fill his head with anger and talk of Jihad. No good –
big trouble."

"What's your brother's name?"

"Sachin Jaskaran Bakri."

"Where does he live?"

"He live with me."

"Have you asked his friends if they know where he's gone?"

"I not trust them. They say Sachin gone on hajj (pilgrimage)
to Mecca, but how could he? His passport was still at home."

"O.K. You stay here for a moment. I'll be back in just a few
minutes and then I'll take you home".

Birchall and Churchill were eagerly awaiting Mike's return.
They could sense immediately that Mike had something from
the interview.

"So, what did you get?" asked Birchall

"I think we're onto a winner, Guv. I think we've found the
identity of the body in the car – it's his brother. We can't be sure
until we've got a DNA sample from this guy so I'll get SOCO to
come along and take a swab before we release him."
Mike then related the story of the missing brother.

"Great. O.K. Mike, get Terry and David to go with you; take
Bakri back to his home and turn it over. Go through everything,
his reading material, photographs, letters, everything. Don't
forget the computer if he has one, have a look at his favourite
sites, e-mails everything and if you feel unsure, bring it here
and let Will Smith have a look at it. We want to know who he
associates with and where he spends his time; who his brother
associated with and what his reading material is."

"Above all, be careful; If there's any chemicals that you're
not sure about – leave them alone and let's get someone to
handle them who knows what they're doing, remember what
Doctor Rajavi said about how dangerous they are", said
Churchill.

Chapter 13

Breakthrough

The room that Sachin Jaskaran Bakri occupied in his brother's home was a muddle of untidy discarded clothing, religious books and pamphlets, heaps of papers all in a foreign script, and an all pervading aroma of garlic. There were DVD discs and computer print-outs and a USB memory stick with 256 megabytes of stored data. These were all put into plastic bags to be translated or examined by forensic experts.

"There's no computer, Mohammed. Does your brother use yours?" asked David.

"I not have computer, he use Internet Café in town. Sachin not like me to see what he was doing."

"Where is your brother's passport?"

"Here, in my case, with his registration – I keep them safe." David took the passport, opening it to reveal Sachin's photograph.

"Is this a good likeness of Sachin?"

"Likeness ? I not understand Likeness."

"Likeness. Has he changed – has he grown a beard or moustache?" David persisted.

"No Sir, likeness OK".

Crenarth Home Office Forensic Science Laboratories responded with some speed in the comparison of DNA samples from Mohammed against the DNA isolated from the body in the burned out car.

"It's one hundred per cent positive. The body is definitely that of Sachin Jaskaran Bakri", announced John Churchill.

"O.K. We need his brother in here as soon as possible. Someone will have to break the news to him and we need him to go through these photographs and identify them", responded Alan Birchall.

"Guv, let me see him. I seem to get on well with him. Let me break the bad news to him. I think I can use it as a lever to get results", proposed Mike.

"O.K Mike, fetch him in."

Mohammed sat at a desk in the corner of the Special Branch office with a cup of steaming hot, sweet tea. His eyes were red and swollen and he was still in a very emotional state having been told of his brother's demise.
Mike sat on the desk facing him.

"I'm sorry to bring you this bad news. The day you came in here to report your brother missing he was already dead. There was nothing you or I could have done about it. But, there's more to tell you about how he died. He was found in a burned out car but he didn't die in a car crash, he was already dead and his body was placed in the car and then deliberately set on fire", said Mike taking it slowly to be as tactful as possible to this grieving brother but needing the explanation to have as much impact as he could manage without causing Mohammed to go into hysteria.

"Who? Who did this thing?" Mohammed wailed.

"That's what we're trying to find out, Mohammed. If you remember, we were asking you about terrorism – about explosives in particular. The reason we asked is because your brother, Sachin, had been involved with the making of explosives, and I'm afraid that's how he died.".

These revelations were having a profound effect on a shocked Mohammed and he again began to wail as tears cascaded down his face. Mike stood beside him and placed a consoling arm around his shoulders. He felt genuinely sorry that such a brutal truth had to be broached. As Mohammed buried his face in his hands he said,

"Sachin my brother, I have failed you. I will pray for your soul", and he produced his subha (prayer beads) and began to mutter to himself.

"Mohammed, it's not you who's failed Sachin, the blame lies with his friends who have led him astray. They are the people who have defiled his body and abandoned him where the rats, foxes and crows could feast on his flesh. We need to find these people and they must be punished."

"Allah will punish them".

"Certainly they will be punished by Allah – but that will be in the next world, not this. Surely your need is to see retribution in this world. I know little of the Islamic teachings but what I do know is that your Qur'an speaks of the law of Moses and the gospel of Jesus that Allah sent down to Muhammad through the angel Gabriel as a guide to mankind, to know right from wrong. Surely His teachings make this wrong?"

"Then fear the Fire whose fuel is men and stones, which is prepared for those who reject Faith...", muttered Mohammed, quoting the Qur'an. " Oh Sachin, why did you let yourself be led astray."

"Who are these people who led him astray, Mohammed?"

"Please, this is very difficult for me, to – how do you say – denounce? – denounce my own kindred".

"Don't you wish to avenge Sachin?"

Mohammed raised his face from his hands to look at Mike as though he was going to reply but there was a silence.

"Mohammed, I want you to look at these photographs. Tell me, do you recognise them?"

He looked at the photographs Mike placed before him then suddenly pushed them away and again buried his face in his hands.

"Who are they, Mohammed?" persisted Mike.

There was a silence again that lasted a full minute before Mohammed finally spoke. Pointing his finger to one of the five in the photograph, he said,

"This is my cousin Javed. He was a good man but he has become – how do you say – a hot-head?. He go to London – I don't know why, but when he came back he had changed. He began to stir up trouble and he was more and more trouble making. He began to teach Sachin his beliefs. I told him to keep away but he wouldn't listen to me. I recognise the others but I don't know them by name."

"Your cousin Javed, what's his full name?"

Mike finally felt he was getting somewhere.

"He is Javed Mustaffa Bakkah".

Mike wrote out the name and showed it to Mohammed who confirmed what was written.

"Where does he live and where does he work?"

"I'm not sure. I think he lives on the Blackwater Estate in a council flat. I don't know where he works – I don't think he has job."

"O.K. Wait here for me. I shall only be a moment or two and then I'll take you back home."

"What has happened to Sachin. Where is his body?"

"It's being held in the mortuary. It can be released to you for funeral arrangements soon."

"Can I see him?"

"Do you really want to see him? You won't recognise him because of the fire. We don't need you to identify him, and if you'll take my advice, don't. Just remember him as he was the last time you saw him".

"I pray Allah has led him to al-janna (paradise)."

Mike went to Jimmy's office next door where John Churchill and Alan Birchall had been listening in to the questioning of Mohammed on the speaker system.

"Well done Mike. I was surprised you took him down that route – where did you learn about the Qur'an?" asked Birchall.

"I don't know much, it's only what I've picked up on the internet. What do we do now about his cousin, Bakkah. Do we pick him up?"

"No. We've not got much against him. It's all   circumstantial and hearsay. I think we'll get Terry to visit the City Council's housing department and find out where Bakkah's living, and someone can go to the DHSS to find out if he's drawing benefit. Then we can set up some obs on him and identify the others. We're fairly sure we're on the right track so we can concentrate all our resources on this. Meanwhile, Will Smith can get digging and find out what's known about Bakkah", answered Churchill.

"I think we've done well, John, to get this far into the enquiry in just a fortnight. We've been very lucky to identify them and I just hope we can build a solid case against them", said Alan Birchall.

Chapter 14

Jihad – Holy war.

Javed Mustaffa Bakkah fuelled by the passion of his inner convictions met again with his friends; countrymen, whom he felt lacked the drive and the religious fervour that Allah demanded of them. It was necessary to continually stimulate and encourage them. They sat together huddled around their bowls of thick, sweet, black coffee, isolated from the remainder of the clientele of the coffee shop.

With furtive glances around them, they spoke in hushed murmurs, ensuring their deliberations were indeed secret.

Javed's heavily pockmarked face, somewhat disguised beneath the straggly beard and moustache, belied his true age. His features were those of a man twice his true age of twenty-eight. His words were hissed through tobacco stained teeth,

"I have again spoken with the Mufti with whom I studied in London. The time has come my brothers to begin the Jihad. Allah decrees that we must further His will."
His words were met with silence from the other three conspirators.

"Come brothers. Are you as the mouse, timid and unworthy of your creed? Ahmed, speak up", Ahmed abruptly put down his coffee and swallowed hard.

Ahmed Al-Bukhari, an Afghan, speaking Pashto and Farsi, had followed his university education for two years in medicine but had finally dropped out to live the easy life on benefits. He had, like many more picked up a basic amount of the English language he needed but despite his obvious talents he lacked a basic endeavour and was easily led.

"But Javed, what would you have us do? Our plan fell apart when Sachin died in the explosion. We agreed that we must lie low until the police let the matter drop", he answered.

"Have you no commitment to our cause? When Sachin died we covered our traces by burning his body. The police haven't even discovered his identity yet. They do not have the intelligence to find us. Surely, because Sachin died we have greater reason to further the cause?"

"What amount of the explosive that Sachin made have we in readiness, Javed?" asked Yuseff. Yuseff Khan was probably the youngest of the group at eighteen but probably the most headstrong. Despite Javed's blood relationship with Sachin, Yuseff had probably been the closest to him and was most affected by his death. He saw Sachin's untimely death as something that should be avenged.

"Enough", snapped Javed.

"You have a plan, Javed?" asked Ahmed.

"I've watched the airport for some time. All the security checks seem to be amongst the passengers. My plan is to begin our action away from the airport."

The group sat in awed silence. As Javed's words sank home Ahmed asked,

"Away from the airport? What do you mean?"

"What do aeroplanes use for fuel?" asked Javed.

"Aviation fuel – paraffin", answered Ahmed.

"Exactly. How is that fuel delivered to the airport?"

"By Tanker?" Ahmed retorted.

"Correct. Now do you see what I'm planning?" and without waiting for an answer Javed continued,

"We hi-jack the tanker on its way to the airport. The driver will be eliminated and I shall take over and drive the vehicle. The security on the supply gates is far less and I will be prepared to crash through the gates if it is necessary."

"But the police on guard at the gates will carry machine guns", said a timid voice. Aashif Sunak, was by far the youngest of the cabal.

"Are you not afraid that you – we – will be shot before we reach the objective?"

It was quite ironic that Aashif should be the timid one as the literal meaning of his name was in fact 'the bold or courageous one' but that irony seemed to be lost on everyone.

"Think about that for a moment...", said Javed,"...Do you think that they will risk firing at a tanker full of aviation fuel? Especially when the driver is captive in the cab, eh? No, they won't and before they can do anything to stop me we'll be inside the airport. I can drive straight up to the embarkation area amongst the passenger planes that are also carrying a full load of fuel. The explosive and the detonator will be in place and there will be such confusion with everyone – baggage handlers and ground staff running everywhere – it should be easy to escape. I can detonate the bomb from a distance with my mobile phone. Can you just see the devastation; petrol tanker, passenger planes and even the terminal in flames?"

He settled back in his chair with a smug contentment about him, savouring the expressions of his friends.

"Allah is great…" said Yuseff, "….hamdulah – praise be to God."

Silence hung over the group as the idea penetrated their minds, but that silence was eventually broken by Aashif saying,

"What happens if we can't get away?"

and Javed snapped, "Allah has promised 70 virgins to all martyrs in al-janna (the garden of paradise)."

Ahmed attempted to pacify Javed by asking,

"What shall we do about this guy, Tariq, who's been following us? He's been trying to make friends with us for ages. Do we let him join us?"

"We don't know anything about him. Is he a true believer? - he might be a police spy. We'll follow him – see where he lives or works. Find out who he sees and what his reasons are for wanting to join us", answered Javed.

Tariq Jamil, still intent upon his infiltration of the group, hoping to facilitate his television expose on terrorism, hung about after devotions. He was more than pleasantly surprised by the softening of attitude of Javed this morning. For the first time there were pleasantries exchanged and Tariq thought that his persistence was eventually paying off. He was more than prepared to put up with the bombardment of questions as he walked with them but he answered each one with a furtive regard choosing to only reveal his intentions much later when he had been accepted.

Already aware of their disenchantment with the views of the elders and the Imam, and still hoping his suspicions that they were an element open to the coercion of terrorists if not already succumbed, he was careful not to compromise himself with probing questions of his own.

Tariq felt he was finally accepted in the group and he tagged along. They reached the bandstand in the park where they seemed to hang around with no particular purpose.

Sie managed a good number of close-up shots from his concealed position with his telephoto lens that had each individual in clear focus.

Aashif made his excuse to leave which saw the break-up of the party.

"Salaam alaikum", said Javed and Tariq answered

"God be with you also."

Tariq left the park and quickly made his way back towards the warehouse studios feeling more than a little pleased with himself and his apparent breakthrough in his quest to penetrate the group.

He allowed himself thoughts of how he would now handle the situation; how he would first consolidate his new relationship before making clear his objectives. Perhaps offer them an appearing on film to further their cause – surely that might be an inducement – even just in silhouette, it had been done before. It was a very touchy subject and he'd have to think hard about the matter and handle it with care.

As he walked, immersed in his thoughts, his mind too full to notice the shadowy figure of Yuseff following a good distance behind. Yuseff watched as Tariq entered the studio and closed the door behind him. He waited allowing Tariq a little time in case this was merely a fleeting visit. As the moments passed it was clear that Tariq had some real purpose in the studio and so Yuseff ventured near to read the brass plaque at the door. 'Golden Salamander Film Company incorporating Salamander Advertising Co Ltd'. He walked away eager to report back to his mentor, Javed.

Chapter 15

Anthrax

Will Smith was busy at the computer trying to break the encryption of the USB memory stick, that he referred to as a gismo, which had been amongst the things gathered from the dead Sashin's room, when he was interrupted by John Churchill,

"Will, can you print the 'photo's from this memory card? Sie has rushed it to me – they're photographs of our suspect, Javed Bakkar, and his mates. Blow them up to A4 size – we've got to get these others identified pronto."

"OK Boss. I'll bring them to you as soon as they're dry."

"Thanks. How are you getting on with that thingamyjig that they picked up at Bakri's home? I can see you're trying something with it on the computer."

"It's encrypted. I've got to break the code; it's just time I need", answered Will as Churchill walked away.

The printer whirred away as Will downloaded and printed one photograph after another which left him with twelve good photographs. Sie had caught most of the group with a full face shot and backed those up with a profile shot too.

"They're good shots Boss", said Will as he spread them out on Churchill's desk.

"Well, we know who this one is – this is our friend Javed Mustaffa Bakkar but who the others are I haven't a clue", answered Churchill.

"That one's a bit long in the tooth to be associating with this bunch. He reminds me of that film star Omar Sharrif", remarked Will pointing his finger to the photograph of Tariq Jamil.

"OK Will. I want you to run a couple of dozen copies off of each and I'll get them circulated around the divisions to see if we can get some identification. We need to get that done as quickly as possible and in the mean time I'll get copies back to Sie so that he can make his comments on them." As an after-thought he continued,

"Run them through the system Will, see if that throws anything up."

Will nodded his head in agreement and left the room.

That same afternoon they all gathered together for one of the regular intelligence update meetings when the photographs were distributed. Mike lifted the photograph of Tariq Jamil for closer inspection.

"I'm sure I've seen this face before but I'm damned if I can remember where", he said aloud.

At that moment Will joined the meeting with an excitement about him that made everyone take notice.

"I've cracked it. I've cracked it." he said as he held the USB gismo aloft. "It's taken some time to break the encryption but I've done it".

"Well? What's it all about?" asked Churchill.

"There's just one word to describe it and that's 'frightening'. It really is frightening. I can only describe it as a terrorists' instruction manual. It's obviously made abroad, probably in Pakistan. I shall have to get Sie to translate everything but anyone can see the diagrams and the chemical ingredients which look to me like instructions on how to make liquid bombs. But, and this is a big 'but', there are also diagrams showing test tubes that look very much like instructions for either chemical or biological bombs", said Will in a very sobering manner.

"I'd rather not bring Sie in for this, he's much more use to us undercover. This sounds as though it's just the ticket for your Doctor Rajavi. He's the chemist and he'll be able to translate for us and give us a professional assessment of what we've got contained on this thing", replied Churchill.

Doctor Rajavi was only too pleased to assist and given the urgency of the matter he responded immediately. He sat before Will's computer screen and translated word for word as Will made his notes in impeccable Pitman's shorthand and Churchill listened intently.

"These are precise instruction for making the explosive Hexamethylene Triperoxide Diamine – HMTD, but you can get all this information from the internet so what's so alarming about this?"

"Oh, you'll see...", said Will, "...We haven't got to the scary bit yet", and he rolled the wheel of the mouse to take the screen to the next phase.

Dr. Rajavi continued to translate the dialogue but suddenly caught his breath as he got to the meat of the message.

"Oh my, you're right, this is frightening. They're proposing biological warfare. It's banned under the Geneva Convention but that means nothing to these animals. They talk of anthrax but that's just a proposal at the moment. I can see their problem in-so-much as they need laboratories and technicians capable of producing the bacteria. They obviously haven't got those in place yet but that problem isn't insurmountable. There'll be laboratories in Pakistan, India and probably Iran that will more than likely do their bidding. The recording talks as though it's certain to be a factor in their Jihad within a very short time. That's a sobering thought."

"So, you believe this is not only feasible but a likely threat in the near future?" said Churchill.

"I'm sorry to say but, yes, I do."

"Well, Thank you Doctor. We're most grateful to you. I must ask you to keep this information to yourself. I'm sure you can imagine what panic this would cause amongst the public; it could lead to violence and racial tension. One last thing before you go - will you please take a look at some photographs for us. Just see if you can identify any of them", said Churchill.

In the main office of the SB, next door, Dr Rajavi was shown the series of photographs now displayed on a large notice board.

"Oh yes, that's definitely one of the two men who first approached me...", pointing to the full face photograph of Javed Bakkar, "...but I don't know who he is."

"That's OK, we know who he is, it's just a matter of tying up loose ends."

"Do you recognise this chap?" asked Mike pointing to the photograph of Tariq Jamil.

"No. Sorry, I don't know him – he looks very suave, not the type to be involved with these others."

"I agree...", replied Mike, "...but never-the-less he is involved somehow. I've seen him before but I can't bring it to mind. Well thank you Dr. Rajavi I'll get someone to run you home."

As Dr. Rajavi left, the meeting was thrown into disarray as David Scott asked,

"What's this mean Boss? Do we now start looking towards biological warfare suits?

"No. Don't let us get this out of proportion. We're dealing with a small group of fanatics, and if Sachin Bakri was anything to go by they're not sophisticated enough to be handling biological stuff. That doesn't mean to say that we can drop our guard. Obviously if we come across anything that we're not sure of then we take proper precautions", answered Birchall.

"It's a frightening prospect but we're not there yet, and hopefully never will be", said John Churchill.

Chapter 16

Sie's headache.

Undercover, Detective Sergeant 'Sie' Asghar was on his second cup of very strong, black, sweet coffee, near the window of the small pavement café. The newspaper that he held in front of him might just as well have been upside down because his attention was outside. The faces in the photographs he had provided were now ingrained in his memory and he could pick them out, even singly, from the throng.

Javed Bakkar was in a huddle with Yuseff Khan in the doorway of a vacant shop which was beginning to take on the look of dereliction and bore the usual fly posters. Bakkar purposely turned his back to the pavement to hide what he was showing Khan. He held the cardboard parcel in the palm of his left hand and threw back the cloth covering with his right to reveal a pair of automatic pistols. The markings of the weapons were indeterminate but appeared to have Czech 9mm ammunition in the two boxes. Yuseff showed his immediate excitement and went to take hold of a weapon but Javed pulled them away with the admonishment, "No. Not here", and he wrapped the cloth over them, carefully looking over his shoulder to make sure he wasn't observed.

"We must take them up to the old quarry where we can practise firing them."

At that moment Javed saw the approaching figure of Tariq Jamil and furtively concealed his parcel of weapons beneath his jacket.

"Salam alaikum", was Tariq's greeting.

"Allahu Akbar", was their response.

"What's that you have under your jacket?" asked a nonchalant Tariq.

"Oh, It's a present for my young nephew. I must keep it hidden."

Tariq instantly sensed the nervous edge to Javed's reply and felt it a lie but decided to let the matter pass without comment.

"I must leave you…", said Javed, "…My nephew awaits his present", and he walked away.

Sie hurriedly left his table at the café and pursued Javed at some distance, conscious of the effort Javed was making to avoid followers. Sie had that unwashed, uncared for appearance and was dressed in torn jeans and dirty sweater that tended to blend with the current youthful fashion.

He took every opportunity to appear unconcerned about Javed, frequently stopping to peer into shop windows but always using the reflections to keep his quarry in view. Javed, on the other hand, was doing his best to employ the little he knew about anti-surveillance techniques, doubling back on himself, entering shops, leaving by different exits, always trying to merge with the crowd, but Sie was above all these tricks – or so he thought.

Suddenly Sie felt a searing pain through his head and as a wave of darkness swept across his conscious mind a hazy vision of a shadowy figure entered his subconscious, then there was oblivion. He fell heavily to the pavement bleeding profusely from his head wound. Javed stood over him, pistol in hand.

The telephone buzzed annoyingly on Detective Superintendent Churchill's desk. He left his seat at the computer screen and snatched up the receiver.
"John Churchill" he said into the mouthpiece.

"Yes Sir, It's Inspector Byrne in communications. It seems we have an Asian man in Crenarth General Hospital. He has head injuries from which he has only just recovered consciousness. Apparently he is asking for you."
A shudder went down John Churchill's spine as he realised it could only be Sie.

"O.K. inspector, leave it with me."
He grabbed his jacket and ran to the next office where Alan Birchall was in conversation with Jimmy Johnson.

"Alan, come with me quickly, we've got a problem."

Alan Birchall could see the deeply concerned feelings etched in Churchill's face.

"What's the matter John?" he asked as they hurried towards the car park.

"It's Sie. Something's happened to him – I don't know what, but he's in hospital with head injuries."

Crenarth General was a fifteen minute drive away under normal conditions but as always in an emergency the traffic always conspires to make life difficult and finding a parking space an extra annoyance. By the time they had waited at the desk to ascertain which ward Sie was in and then trudged through the corridors, it was almost a quarter of an hour later that they reached ward 24, next to the intensive care unit. They pushed open the double swing doors and stepped into the ward.

A white coated medic barred their way,

"What are you doing here?" he asked.

"I am Detective Superintendent Churchill and this is Detective Superintendent Birchall", he said producing his warrant card. "I understand from the admissions clerk that you have someone here by the name of Saied Asghar who's been admitted with head injuries".

The inflexion in the sentence made it a question.

"Yes, that's correct but I'm afraid Mr Asghar is in a confused state and I can't allow you to question him."

"Who are you?" asked Churchill.

"I'm Dr.Cox and I'm in charge of this ward and of Mr Asghar's welfare."

"Well, Doctor Cox, Mr. Asghar has asked to see me urgently and I'd be obliged if you would kindly show me to his bed. This is a matter of national security and although I respect your authority and concern here I must insist on seeing Mr. Asghar", said Churchill.

"Alright gentlemen but you have to understand that he has suffered a very severe blow to the head and he still appears to be somewhat concussed, so please, don't put him under stress and keep your visit as short as possible. He's behind the screens at the end of the ward. If you'll follow me I'll take you to him."

"What the hell's happened to you Sie?" asked Churchill as he looked at the bandages that were still weeping blood. Doctor Cox was writing on the clip board that had hung from Sie's bed.

"Doctor, would you be kind enough to leave us for a moment or two. This is Official Secrets Act stuff", said Churchill. The doctor looked wide eyed in astonishment and meekly withdrew.

"Sie, what's happened?" he repeated.

Sie looked up at Churchill, lifted his arm across his face to shield his eyes from the light and said,

"I slipped up Guv. He got the drop on me. It was Bakkar. I'd kept him under surveillance for some time and he'd got a parcel that he was trying to keep hidden. I tried to follow him but he was crafty. I thought I'd got the measure of him but he must have sussed me. He led me down an alley off the main street and disappeared inside a doorway. I thought I'd concealed myself and was waiting for him to reappear but he must have come out through another exit and dropped on me from behind. I don't know much more; someone found me lying in a pool of blood. It must have been Bakkar; I don't know what he hit me with but I'm seeing stars."

Sie sank back into his pillow and drifted off into unconsciousness. Churchill swiftly called Doctor Cox who reproachfully said,

"This is what I feared. He has suffered a severe concussion and should remain quiet and undisturbed. Your questioning, regardless of how important you see it, is harmful to his recovery and that's why I didn't want you to question him. I must ask you both to leave".

Churchill was suitably admonished but said to Birchall as they left,

"Sie's made of strong stuff. He'll be o.k. We've got to decide what we're going to do about Bakkar now."

In the car, travelling back to the office, John Churchill said to Alan Birchall,

"What are your feelings Alan. They've sussed Sie so our cover's blown. What do you think ought to be our next move?"

"Well, I know it's difficult because all we've got is circumstantial. If only we could find where they've been making their explosive we'd be ok.

"Yes, but we don't know where, do we? I know it's not an ideal situation but I think we've got to arrest them. Pull them all in and chance it that we can strengthen what we've got with interviews and searches of their homes. What are your views?"

"It begins to look as though we have no option. I think we'd better get back to the office and have words with the CPS."

Chapter 17

MI5

Javed Bakkar looked quizzically at the others.

"We're being watched".

He left a silence to give stress to his words then continued,

"Someone has talked; who's the blabber-mouth?", and he watched the facial expressions of the others for some sign of guilt.

"Why, what makes you say that Javed", asked Ahmed Al-Bukhari.

"Because I was followed. I knew – something told me, call it a sixth sense – that I was being followed, so I ducked in and out of shops, doubled back on myself, stood in a queue and then suddenly walked away. Just one face was staying with me whatever I did so I went into an alley and found a printer's shop. I entered by the main door and found my way through the workshop and out onto the main street. I circled around and came back to the alley and there he was, waiting amongst the garbage bins. I crept up behind him and 'wham'… I hit him over the head and left him lying there. He'll have a headache to remember for quite some time when he wakes up."

"I'm sure none of us has said anything Javed. This has got to be something to do with this guy, Tariq, the one I followed to the warehouse where they make the films. I don't like him, none of us knew him when he turned up here and yet he's tried his best to nurture our friendship and be accepted. There's something wrong about him. It's time to find out what he's doing; who he really is and who he's working for. For all we know he might be a police spy," said Yuseff.

"I tend to agree with young Yuseff here. We don't know who he is and I don't like him either", said Ahmed. Aashif as usual kept very quiet.

"That must wait. I've other plans", insisted Javed.

Alan Birchall replaced the receiver on its cradle and leant back in his chair. His fingertips came together with his fingers splayed open in that figurative pose that he adopted when he needed to concentrate his thoughts. His conversation with the CPS left him in no doubt that although the suspicion was there to arrest the suspects there was no hard evidence against any one of them.

The encrypted USB was only evidence against Sachin Bakri who was now dead. He now had to make up his mind whether to order the arrests on suspicion alone, and chance that the interviews would provide the necessary evidence for a prosecution. He knew that the new laws on detention in connection with terrorism gave him the authority but he also knew that without some solid evidence, he was out on a limb.

The most important consideration in this dilemma was the safety of the public. Could he continue to play a waiting game – especially now that Sie had been rumbled – not even knowing what diabolical scheme they had in mind.

John Churchill and Terry Jones had made it quite clear that they felt the decision had been forced upon them to act. He made up his mind that he'd recommend to the ACC (Assistant Chief Constable) that they would arrest the suspects – after all, the Chief had the ultimate say in the matter.

He was about to lift the internal 'phone to carry out his intentions when suddenly the secure line rang. He snatched up the receiver and spoke.

"Alan Birchall"

"Yes, hello Alan, this is Simon Carlisle, at the Security Service. Are we on a secure line?"

"Hello Simon, Yes, we're secure. Have I met you?"

"No. I don't think we've met, at least I don't remember meeting you. Look, forget the pleasantries, I understand you're facing a problem with a terrorist cell. My department have been monitoring your situation from the messages you've sent us and we've been doing the background checks – in fact I've only just put down the 'phone to GCHQ – and it seems you've definitely got an active little cell there. I think the time has come for us to come and take a look."

"Well, Simon, it seems that our 'situation', as you put it, has run on a pace since our last report to you. We've had the Met boys here working with us for a few days. Unfortunately, one of our undercover men has been taken to hospital having been assaulted by these terrorists and we fear that his cover's been blown. I've just been taking CPS advice and have virtually concluded that the time has come to arrest them. We're aware that the evidence is thin and very circumstantial but unless we act now, they may fear discovery and be scared into doing their diabolical worst. So, do you think it worth your while rushing up here now we've gone this far?"

"I think I'd better come anyway. I would however appreciate it if you would hang fire for twenty-four hours before you rush in to arrest these men. I'd like to come and assess the situation and, perhaps, offer my advice. What do you say?"

"Well, I'm hardly in a position to say yes. Come up by all means but with our man in hospital and the prospect of these men committing some terrible explosion and killing or maiming people, I hardly think we can afford to wait much longer."

"Look, twenty-four hours isn't going to make much difference, is it?"

"Simon, come up tomorrow by all means – I'll be here but I'm making no promises because, when all's said and done, it's not my decision to make – it's the Chief's. All that I can say is that I'll make him aware of your request."

At that moment the office door opened and John Churchill entered – just as Alan replaced the receiver.

"Damn and blast", grimaced Alan and John looked quizzically at him,

"What's the matter?"

"It's the Security Service, a chap called Simon Carlisle. He's coming up tomorrow and he wants us to delay any action on these suspects until he's been and assessed the situation."

"Well, my view is that we should carry on as we proposed. There's nothing that he can say or do that's going to help us if we allow these fanatics time to carry out an attack. We're the ones to carry the can. You might detect some antagonism in my voice – the reason is we, the Met that is, are continually frustrated by these Hooray Henrys who think they're somehow superior. Have you spoken with the Assistant Chief Constable yet?"

"No. That's what I was about when I received that call."

"O.K. well, do it now and whilst you're speaking with him, let me offer him some candid advice too."

Alan could almost feel the heat rising in John Churchill as the man clearly contemplated this as interference by the Security Service.

"What advice will that be, John?"

"That they've had as much time to respond to your problem as we, the Met, have. Whatever they've been doing in the background, hasn't exactly been of much assistance and at the end of the day they can't do any more than we're doing. Now they want you to delay action whilst they catch up with what's happening. My advice is to strike now and not give these buggers the chance to do us any harm."

Alan Birchall listened intently to what John Churchill was saying and then posed the question,

"Does this mean to say that when this Simon Carlisle turns up tomorrow we're going to have a confrontational problem ?"

"Oh no, Alan. I shall work with him – and you – as I've always done. There's been this – what shall I call it – not a barrier but certainly a feeling of antipathy or animosity if not just plain rivalry – between the Met SB and the Security Service for years. It all boils down to an egotistical attempt at preservation of their status above us when we're all doing the same job and have the same abilities. No, there'll be no confrontation. I perhaps shouldn't have said anything."

"O.K, well, It's perhaps as well to know these things. My advice to the ACC will be that we carry on and go for the arrests. My concerns are exactly the same as yours that if we delay we may give them the chance to carry out some atrocity which would then leave us with terrible regrets."

Chapter 18

Jahannam – Fire of Hell.

Javed outlined his plans to the others,

"If we've been betrayed we must act quickly. We can deal with the traitor afterwards."

The hot wired Ford Mondeo headed out through the suburbs to the airport with Javed at the wheel. Ahmed sat beside him holding the bag containing the four bottles of Sachin's explosive delicately and warily upon his knee, trying his best not to jolt them. There was an all pervading nervous tension within the car.

"He is God; there is no God but He. He is the knower of the invisible and the visible; he is the all-compassionate, the all-caring", muttered Ahmed reciting the Sura, and continued, "Oh God, if I worship you for fear of hell, burn me in hell, and if I worship you in hope of paradise, exclude me from paradise; but if I worship you for your own sake, deny me not your eternal beauty", quoting Attar's Memoirs of the Saints.

"Ahmed, do you fear jihad?" asked Javed seeing his sweat soaked brow.

"No, Javed, but I prepare my soul for al-janna (paradise)", he replied.

"In-sha'a-llah (God willing) we shall all meet in al-janna (the garden of paradise). Remember, all of you, the hadith (tradition) assures us that a Muslim who dies whilst fighting for Islam secures for himself entrance to heaven without undergoing the ordeal of the Day of Judgement. Remember my brothers, jihad (holy war or struggle) is the sixth pillar of Islam."

Aashif sat quietly in the back seat with Yuseff, contemplating his prayer beads and quietly reciting to himself the ninety-nine names of Allah.

Javed stopped at a lay-by about three quarters of a mile from the airport. It was a route he'd watched over for a period of days and now he sat back to wait with the engine quietly idling. After only twenty minutes or so he saw, in his rear-view mirror, the approach of the target he was waiting for. He put the gear lever into first gear and sat with the clutch pedal depressed.

Suddenly he let the clutch out and accelerated from the lay-by into the path of a fuel tanker. The tanker's brakes squealed and the tyres left black marks on the road surface as it slid into the rear offside corner of the Mondeo and pushed it forwards. It was a carefully calculated manoeuvre by Javed that caused the collision to occur without too much damage.

Both vehicles stopped and Javed watched as the tanker driver climbed down from his cab obviously furious at the manner in which the Mondeo had left the lay-by without checking that the road was clear. As he approached Javed's car he reached into his overall pocket and brought out his mobile 'phone, clearly intending to report the accident and alert his employers.

Javed sprang from his vehicle and confronted the tanker driver with the pistol which immediately gave the angry driver an understanding of the 'accident' and he realised it was an ambush. Javed rushed to him and pushed the gun into his ribs, at the same time snatching the 'phone from his hand.

Ahmed, Yuseff and Aashif quickly joined Javed and the tanker driver was roughly handled to the kerbside where he was out of sight of any other driver who might pass by. There, he was ordered to remove his overall. Quite terrified at what was happening to him, he quickly obeyed. He was ordered at gun point to climb into the passenger seat of the tanker and his hands were taped behind his back with broad insulation tape that Yuseff produced from his pocket.

Yuseff squeezed into the passenger seat alongside the driver. Javed turned to Ahmed and said, as he struggled into the overalls that had been taken from the driver,

"I'm going to place the explosive onto the fuel tank and tape it in position with the electrical detonator. I'll drive the tanker, Yuseff will be with me in the tanker cab, you must drive the car. I want you to wait in the car-park near the 'arrivals' terminal. Park as close to the exit as you can and if they try to move you pretend the car's broken down. It will give us sufficient time to drive the tanker to where it will cause most harm, and we'll escape and find you before I detonate the explosive. When the tanker explodes the jinn (a fiery spirit) will cause such confusion and we shall simply exit the car park and get back to Crenarth to dump the car. Do you understand?"

"I understand, brother. We'll meet in the car park in-sha'a-llah (God willing). Al-hamdu li-Llah (Praise to God)" answered Ahmed.

Ahmed and Aashif drove off in the Mondeo leaving Javed to drive the fuel tanker and Yuseff to control the unhappy delivery driver. Javed climbed up into the driver's seat and looked for the clip-board holding the delivery note which denoted high octane fuel. He started the engine, engaged gear and pushed off the little handbrake lever that created a hiss of escaping compressed air and moved off very steadily towards the supply gate that he had previously reconnoitred. At the security gate he stopped and pushed the captive tanker driver down into the foot-well where he couldn't be seen. Anticipating the gate-man's demand he wound down the window and handed down the clip-board together with the real driver's identity tag. The guard seemed to accept the documents without question and opened up the first security gate. Javed drove inside and the gate closed behind him. The tension was high and the perspiration began to stand out on his brow. He drew his sleeve across his forehead. A second uniformed guard joined the first and took the clip board, peeled off the top copy of the delivery note and signed the copy underneath, but before handing the clip-board back to Javed he walked around the length of the vehicle to the passenger side of the cab.

"Who are you ?" he asked Yuseff.

"I'm the temporary driver's mate; just learning the job", he answered coolly.

"O.K. wait there whilst I check", the guard said and turned away to return to his gate-house.

A solitary police officer stood beyond the next security gate holding an MP5 light machine carbine across his chest.

"Javed, what shall we do? He's suspicious. I can see him on the 'phone and he keeps looking back at me as though he's describing me to someone."

"Hold your nerve Yuseff. Let's see what he has to say when he returns."

In readiness of a problem he put the vehicle into gear and kept the clutch depressed. He watched as the guard left the telephone and walked to the security gate but instead of opening the gate he spoke with the police officer. Sensing that something was about to happen to prevent their entry, Javed released the clutch and pressed down on the accelerator and the big diesel engine roared into life and the tanker shot forward, smashing through the gate. The police officer jumped back to avoid injury but before he could regain his balance and bring up his gun to fire, the cab of the tanker was past him and he hesitated to fire lest he hit the tank causing the fuel to erupt into an inferno.

Javed roared through the maze of ancillary buildings and parked vehicles making towards the main concentration of activity where there were several aircraft being loaded from the baggage trailers. One aircraft had a tractor attached to the nose-wheel as though in readiness to be pushed out and made ready for take-off.

Suddenly there was an ear-splitting wail of a two-tone siren that filled the air. Javed drove the tanker to the front of the aircraft that had the tractor attached which placed him immediately in front of the huge glass walled embarkation lounge. The hiss of the air-brakes was almost imperceptible in the din from the siren as Javed flicked the handbrake lever.

"Run for it Yuseff. We'll grab one of those electric baggage tolleys over there", pointing towards the other aircraft being loaded. They jumped from the vehicle leaving their prisoner to fend for himself. They both ran to the nearest electric vehicle and jumped aboard. It was as if time was standing still; no-one in the vicinity was making any move to intercept them, almost as if the siren was an everyday occurrence that everyone dismissed as another false alarm.

The electric baggage truck wasn't fast, but even so, it was running pace. Yuseff picked up two yellow fluorescent jackets from the truck that the baggage handlers wore and they put them on over their jackets giving them the appearance of bona fide airport workers.

Back near the entry gate it was pandemonium with no-one seeming to have any idea about what they should be doing. Javed swung the electric trolley around the rear of the gate-house to the pedestrian exit. A uniformed gate-man came through a doorway close by and before he realised what had happened Yuseff grabbed him around his throat and pressed the barrel of his automatic into his ribs. He pressed him against the wall so that he was out of sight of his companions.

"Keep quiet or I'll kill you. Do you understand ?" he said and the man nodded.

"Don't hurt me, please", choked the gate-man.

"Keep quiet. Do as you're told and you won't get hurt."

Javed was holding his mobile 'phone in his left hand frantically punching numbers. Nothing was happening and he looked up at Yuseff in frustration, and said,

"The detonator. It isn't working."

He worked like a demon repeatedly punching the trigger number into his 'phone until he realised the battery symbol was showing low battery. His mind was in turmoil – he had planned everything to that last detail only to be thwarted by a low battery in his mobile 'phone. Suddenly there was an ear splitting 'boom' as the noise of the explosion echoed around and a huge ball of fire and smoke rose high above the buildings. Glass flew from the shattered windows of the observation lounge causing horrendous injuries to those inside.

Another siren wailed from the airport's own fire-engine. Every aspect of the explosion and fire was hidden from Javed and Yuseff but they looked at each other in smug satisfaction. At the scene of the fire the explosion had punctured a huge hole in the fuel tanker and burning fuel was awash on the concrete of the airport apron, engulfing the tractor unit and the nose of its Boeing 727 aircraft.

As realisation dawned the emergency chutes were deployed from the centre and rear of both sides of the aircraft and terrified passengers began to slide to safety. As they jostled amongst themselves to replace footwear or find their partners and family members, stewards fought to shepherd them well clear of the danger. The heat from the massive fire was too intense for anyone to contemplate moving either the tractor unit or the aircraft and within a very short time the tyres of the tractor and the nose-wheel of the plane were spewing dense black smoke as they burned. It seemed only seconds before the three fire tenders reached the scene, each crew ran out their hoses and a vast carpet of foam was laid to extinguish the flames. The fuel tanker burned so fiercely it sent huge clouds of choking black smoke up in a plume that reached high into an otherwise clear sky.

Inside the terminal building the waiting passengers were relaxing, drinking their coffee and eating their snacks in a contented mood anticipating their own flights as Javed brought the fuel tanker to a halt. No-one really took much notice until someone suddenly shouted in excitement seeing two men jump from the vehicle waving automatic pistols. As is the nature of the inquisitive human mind, the window became crowded with people anxious to see what was going on. It was the last place that anyone would want to be as the explosion shattered the glass and sent shards scything through the air and tearing into flesh. Blood soaked clothing and furniture and the whole lounge was the epitome of a war zone.

Pushing the frightened gate-man in front of him, Yuseff pushed the rear door of the gate-house open and went inside. Through the glass window of the internal door Javed could see a second man sitting at a console and working feverishly between telephone and switches. They watched as the outer gate swung open to admit a police car with blue flashing lights that then sped into the airport.

"What did he do to open the gate?" hissed Yuseff to his prisoner. When there was no immediate reply Yuseff angrily forced the weapon deep into the man's ribs.

"What did he do to open the gate?" he repeated.

"Let me breathe, please", the man implored, desperately clawing at Yuseff's arm to release his throat, then spluttered,

"It's that green button on the console",

The gate-keeper at the console, a man of almost retirement age, swivelled around as the door burst open. He gasped as he saw the guns and his friend held in a vice like grip. He staggered to his feet, his brow heavy with beads of perspiration, holding his chest with one hand and supporting himself on the desk with the other. His face turned florid and suddenly he fell to the floor suffering a heart attack. Yuseff released his grip on his prisoner and said, "Help your friend", and he stepped forward and pressed the green button.

The gate swung open. Javed and Yuseff rushed from the building making for the open gate. A uniformed police officer approaching the gate house saw the fugitives and realised that they were somehow connected with the explosion and shouted a warning to stop but Yuseff turned in his flight and fired in the general direction of the officer. Two shots rang out in response from the officer's carbine one round ricocheting off the metal gate and the second hitting Javed in the muscle of his thigh, bowling him over.

Yuseff hesitated then turned to face the officer and in the same instant brought up his weapon in careful aim and fired two rounds in rapid succession. The officer was hit squarely in the chest and although his protective vest saved his life the impact knocked him backwards off his feet in excruciating pain. His carbine clattered to the ground.

Javed and Yuseff arrived at the car park panting and out of breath. Javed limping heavily, obviously in excruciating pain from the bullet wound, and Yuseff supporting his injured friend. Ahmed and Aashif were diligently waiting and were frightened at the sight of Javed, injured and soaked in blood. As they sped away from the car park Yuseff tore a broad strip of material from his shirt and bound it tightly around Javed's thigh.

"Steady Ahmed. Drive steadily, Don't attract attention to yourself", grimaced Javed who then lapsed into a pained silence as they drove away.

"What's happened, Javed?", Ahmed asked presently,

"You're very quiet. Have we failed? Surely we heard the explosion?"

"I thought the detonator had failed. My mobile 'phone battery was low and I thought we'd failed, but suddenly it exploded. We couldn't see it but it must have been like jahannam (the fire of hell), the beast that meets the sinners on the Day of Judgement as the Sura tells us. Allah will look kindly upon us."

Emergency Ambulances, Fire Service tenders and Police cars were screaming along in the opposite direction to join the bedlam of the airport. Aashif was feeling extremely nervous and was twisted around in his seat anxious to assure himself that they weren't being followed, his fingers working his worry beads.

"What's this ahead?" said Ahmed aloud, to no one in particular, as he saw the traffic queueing. Javed lifted his head from contemplating his injured thigh and briefly caught sight of a blue flashing light in the far distance.

"Road Block...", he shouted. "....Road Block. Swing around, go back about half a mile, I know another way."

Ahmed braked hard and slowed the Mondeo but the tight turn caused the vehicle to lean over violently and Yuseff fell heavily against Javed's injured leg causing him to shout out in pain. Ahmed regained control of the vehicle and pushed hard on the accelerator, all the time keeping his eye on the rear-view mirror anticipating that a police vehicle would come tearing after them.

"Take the next on the right, Ahmed. It's a narrow lane so watch out for vehicles coming the other way. It's a long way round but it takes us around the back of the Blackwater Estate. We'll ditch the car before we reach the houses. Find somewhere; a field or somewhere quiet.
There's a can of petrol in the boot; we'll fire it so there's no evidence left to connect us", said Javed.

"But you're wounded, Javed. How will you walk ?" asked Ahmed.

"Just do as I say", snapped Javed.
Ahmed drove the car through an open gateway into a field where they were hidden by a tall Hawthorne hedge. As the vehicle came to a halt they all alighted, looking around them to make sure they weren't observed. Yuseff went to the car boot and found the can of petrol.

"Stand well back", he said as Ahmed supported Javed and Aashif looked on, the contents of the can were splashed through the interior of the car. Tossing the empty can inside the vehicle Yuseff then stood well back as he took matches from his pocket. Just a single match thrown in the direction of the vehicle was sufficient to light the heavy petrol vapours and there was an almighty 'whoosh' as it ignited. The four quickly walked away, Ahmed and Yuseff either side of Javed supporting him. In the far distance they could hear the wail of sirens on the main road.

"We must get you some treatment for the wound", said Ahmed as he looked at Javed's leg. His trousers were slowly becoming soaked in blood.

"No. Now's the time to deal with the traitor, Tariq. If we return to our homes they might be waiting for us. We've got to find out how much he's said. Take us to the warehouse, Yuseff. I can wash the wound and bind it properly when we get there", said Javed through gritted teeth.

The rising column of smoke from the burning car caught the attention of the officers manning the road block on the main road. Nothing could be ignored in dealing with an incident of terrorism and officers were despatched to investigate. It was too much to believe this was just a coincidence – a burning car so close to the airport.

A dog handlers were called to the scene and a scent was quickly established on this country road. The scent was strong and the Alsatian pulled hard on his leash.

Chapter 19

The siege.

It was late afternoon and the daylight was fading fast when the four men reached the warehouse. The lights were burning brightly inside the building but there was little noise inside. They stood outside huddled against the wall to make themselves less visible from the windows. Javed produced his handgun. He hesitated momentarily before thrusting it into the hands of Ahmed who seemed reluctant to take the weapon.

"What do we want these for?"

"They are our insurance…", Javed answered, "….Remember, we are lost if this spy, Tariq, has exposed us. We are warriors and this is our fight for Islam."

"I'm not happy with this Javed. I don't particularly like guns, just look what has happened to your leg", said Ahmed.

They were at the point of entering the building and it wasn't a time for argument and Javed took the weapon back. He was in severe pain from his wound but was fiercely determined to carry on. Aashif said nothing and seemed to be shivering.

Ahmed looked around and felt a sudden panic as in the distance he saw a small group of police officers moving purposely in their direction. A huge black Alsation was tugging at it's lead – Aashif's realisation of the predicament and his fear of dogs, made him wet himself.

Yuseff tried the door and found it unlocked. He hastily pushed it open and peered cautiously inside. The doorway gave access to a large workplace with scenery stacked to one side, coil upon coil of cable piled before it. A forklift truck was parked only feet inside the doorway and an electric hoist dangled from a gantry. To the left there were five wooden steps that led to a wooden door with a small window which showed a light inside the room which seemed to be an office. Beyond the steps were stacked numerous packing cases. Visibility was poor as there were no windows in this area and the lights were off.

He slid in through the doorway and hesitated to listen. All that he could hear were female voices. A telephone rang and made his pulse race even more.

He beckoned the others to follow him inside and, placing a finger on his lips, he indicated to them to be very quiet. He pointed directly at Ahmed who was still at the door, looking back towards the approaching police, and motioned to him to hide behind the packing cases. Javed grabbed Aashif's arm and dragged him behind the forklift truck.

"Yuseff, we're discovered. The police are following us", Ahmed hissed as loud as he dare.

Yuseff turned towards the steps ignoring Ahmed's warning and slowly and very carefully he placed his weight on the bottom step almost anticipating a creak from the timber, but none came. He began to climb and on the fifth step he gingerly took hold of the handle to the door and twisted. There was a 'click' as the catch operated and he stopped, holding his breath, as he listened to hear if the noise had disturbed anyone. He tried to peer through the frosted glass of the small window in the door but could see nothing.

In the brightness of overhead fluorescent lighting, Janice was sat engrossed in a huge spread-sheet on her desk, her mind totally given to the columns of figures. Angie was on her knees searching through the cardboard boxes of papers under the bench. Several small piles of invoices and order forms about her were the result of her endeavour to put them in some semblance of order. At the far corner of the office was the small switchboard where Helen sat, balancing the telephone receiver in the crook of her neck, whilst using both hands to operate the keyboard of her computer.

Tariq sat, shirt-sleeved, legs crossed, with his back to the door, a clip-board with a ream of papers attached, on his knee. He lifted his coffee mug to his lips but he had neglected it for so long that the coffee had gone cold. He was just replacing the mug on the desk as the door suddenly bust open.

The noise startled him and the cold coffee spilled onto his trousers. He turned to see a man inside the doorway adopting a crouched, menacing posture, holding a pistol in his two outstretched hands. In almost the same moment his emotions

120

went through shock and fear to puzzlement as he recognised Yuseff. Helen let out a terrified scream and let the telephone handset fall from her shoulder to dangle over the edge of the desk. Tariq, in his astonishment jumped to his feet but the threat of the firearm pointed directly at him subdued any rash action on his part.

"Who else is there in the building ?" shouted Yuseff at no-one in particular. Panic had gripped the throat of Janice and although she tried to reply she found she couldn't speak.

"Who else is in the building ?" repeated Yuseff. Tariq recovered his nerve and answered,

"No one. The camera men and the sound boys have gone home. The warehouse chap left mid afternoon and the old boy that locks up won't be here until about seven. Yuseff, what's this all about? Put the gun away, please you're frightening everyone".

Javed followed, limping heavily, into the office brandishing his weapon, as Aashif stood in the open doorway and Ahmed carefully tilted the window blind to look outside. The fading light made it difficult but there seemed to be shadowy figures in the street that immediately registered as policemen. He whispered to Javed

"We're surrounded Javed. What are we going to do?"

"Make sure the doors are fast so no-one can get in here," and Aashif turned to place the heavy wooden bar that made the doors doubly secure.

Yuseff produced a handful of long cable-ties that he had found on the forklift and he ushered the girls and Tariq into the corner whilst he re- arranged chairs along one side of the office. He motioned Tariq first into a chair and roughly pulled his arms behind him and fastened them together with the cable ties. His protests were ignored. Next he placed a cable-tie around each ankle, fastening him to the legs of the chair.

Janice, Angie and Helen were treated in similar fashion until they were all four, totally incapable of movement. They whimpered in fear and Helen cried uncontrollably.

"Shut up. Stop your noise or you'll be gagged" said Yuseff as he struck her across the face with the back of his hand.

Aashif gasped, "Yuseff, stop, please. Surely we don't wage Jihad on women", showing almost compassionate concern for Hellen.

No-one it seems had noticed the telephone handset still dangling from the desk.

Javed eased himself into a swivel chair and leant back. His head was swimming and the sweat stood out on his brow. The throbbing of his wounded thigh was becoming unbearable and he continually fought to focus his mind on his problems. He drew his sleeve across his forehead to soak up the sweat as it ran into his eyes yet the stinging sensation to his eyes was the least of his concerns.

Chapter 20

Hostages.

"**W**hy are you doing this Javed ?" asked Tariq.

"You know better than anyone" shouted Yuseff and struck Tariq a full blooded blow to his face from a clenched fist. Tariq could do nothing to avoid the blow which drove his lower lip into his teeth. The blood began to trickle from his mouth. He appealed again to Javed,

"Javed, please. We have done nothing to warrant this. Please, Javed, stop this before someone really gets hurt."

Yuseff pressed the muzzle of his pistol into Tariq's cheek saying, "Spy. Traitor", and then struck him across the side of the head with his gun. The blood began to ooze copiously from the wound and ran down his ear to stain his collar.

"Stop, stop, you coward", shouted Angie in anger at Yuseff and Helen screamed. Janice said in almost hushed tones,

"Angie, be quiet. Don't give them an excuse to hurt us".

"They are cowards…", said Angie ignoring Janice's plea. "….It's always the same with cowards they think they're brave, wielding guns and hitting people who can't defend themselves."

"Aashif, find me some tape to bind their mouths", said Yuseff. Aashif was showing a marked degree of reluctance in the whole situation but he went back to the forklift and returned with a roll of wide, sticky, packing tape which Yuseff snatched from him.

Ahmed took hold of Javed's shoulder to draw his attention, saying quietly,

"Javed, you are losing control. Yuseff is getting out of hand, he's taking over. The police are here and Yuseff's going to get us all killed".

Angie noticed the distraction and winked at Janice and nodded towards the telephone handset that still dangled from the desk, as much as to say, 'That's why I said what I did, hoping that there's still someone listening on the 'phone', but of course her mouth was taped.

Javed limped to Tariq's side and said in a quiet, controlled voice,

"You've betrayed us. Why?"

Tariq vigorously shook his head. Javed pulled the tape from Tariq's mouth and asked,

"What are you trying to say?"

"I have not betrayed you my brother. I've said nothing about you to anyone."

"We've been followed and spied upon so someone has to be responsible for betraying us. You're the only one outside our group who knows anything about us. It has to be you."

"No, Javed. Please, you must believe me, I have not betrayed you. If you were betrayed it has come from within your group."

The sudden deafening 'crack' of a pistol being fired near the side of Tariq's head made his head ring and his ears hurt. His heart missed a beat.

"You lie you whimpering cur, you worthless dog. The next bullet will be in your brain", snarled Yuseff. Javed turned and pushed Yuseff's gun aside,

"Yuseff, you're making me angry. Have you no sense? that shot will have been heard outside."

"But, Javed, he lies. He must not be allowed to get away with it."

"Give the gun to me, Yuseff.

"No. I must have a weapon. I promise I won't fire again unless I have to."

"Well, cool it. Let me speak to Tariq again and don't interrupt."

Tariq was still shaking his head as his eardrums reverberated and the pain felt almost as though a knife was being forced through his ear. The sticky tape still dangled from one side of his mouth.

"You protest that you did nothing to betray us but I still cannot believe you. You were too eager to work your way into our midst and your motives have been suspect from that very first day. It's been obvious that you don't have the passionate belief in Jihad that we have so it's obvious that you tried to infiltrate for some other reason. Are you a police spy?"

"No. No. No, Javed, I wanted to gain your trust, yes, but not to betray you. I'm a film maker – that's why I'm here, and I wanted to make a film – something that would be sympathetic to your beliefs and perhaps help the people of the West to understand your feelings and beliefs", said Tariq looking straight into Javed's face and using as much conviction as possible.

"That's so easy for you to say now, but you made no such mention whenever we saw you."

"But it is true, Javed. I couldn't put it to you immediately because you would have rejected it as you tried to reject me. I thought we were just beginning to accept each other and I would have sounded you out about the film quite soon. I've never, at any time, said or done anything to deliberately put you at risk, believe me".

"Leave him, Javed. Let's get your leg sorted out. There's a medical cabinet in the corner", pleaded Ahmed.

Javed was quite faint and his thigh felt hard as though the muscle was in spasm and it burned almost as though on fire. He felt quite sick and weak.

Ahmed had reconnoitred the warehouse floor and discovered a washroom and toilets situated behind the office.

"Javed let me wash your wound. There disinfectant in the washroom," but Javed was too concerned about their predicament.

"I didn't anticipate this situation. I never intended that we should take hostages but I think it may be our only way out. The police are surrounding us and we may have to bargain our way out."

Ahmed persevered and gradually led the injured Javed to the washroom. He released his belt and lowered his trousers whilst Ahmed found him a chair. Ahmed filled a sink with hot water and splashed a small amount of disinfectant into the water. From a roll of lint taken from the first-aid cabinet, he tore off a piece to use as a swab to clean the wound.

"We're lucky, Javed, the bullet's gone through your leg. It's made a bit of a mess but at least it's not still in there. You're lucky, It's muscle damage and there's no arterial damage. There's plenty of gauze and dressings in the cabinet, I'll bandage it once it's clean but we need to get you to a hospital. You need antibiotics."

"No. No hospitals – even if we manage to get out of here the police will be watching hospitals and chemists shops."

Ahmed gently dabbed the wound with the cotton wool and disinfectant causing the raw flesh to sting unbearably. The exit wound was by far the largest and it had to be packed with gauze and cotton.

Although Ahmed was taking considerable care in covering the wound and applying a tight bandage, he knew that the bullet would have dragged small strands of cotton fabric into the flesh that would harbour bacteria. Javed must somehow have antibiotics.

Mrs Lottie Calver, the company secretary of Fairburn Sunblock Co. Ltd., was in the middle of a conversation with Helen Cross about the forthcoming TV commercial. It was a conversation that she would have preferred to have had with Janice Thomas as she wanted to push the deadlines, but it seems she wasn't available. Helen was just running through schedules from a list when suddenly there was a piercing scream and it seemed that the telephone handset banged against something.

"Helen – Miss Cross, what's the matter? What's happening?" but there was no answer. Shouting and screaming was all she could hear and she felt gripped with panic.

Lottie listened hard but the noise was difficult to understand. A female voice was pleading to someone to stop – but stop what? Then someone said something about a gun. For some short time there was relative silence but then the distinctive 'crack' of a gun being fired.

Lottie took a deep breath and sat back in her chair staring at her own telephone handset, trying to make heads or tales of what was happening. It was certainly confusing, after all, she was dealing with a film company – was this all part of some scene that was being filmed? What should she make of it? What should she do?

The 'phone line was still open and she could hear background noise of people moving about and speaking but she could hear nothing more of the conversation. She hesitated and thought long and hard – should she telephone the police? Was she going to appear an awful fool if what she had heard was part of a film scene? But if it was part of a scene why had her telephone conversation been so abruptly cut and why was the handset not replaced?

"Police. Emergency", said the operator.

"Yes. My name is Lottie Calver. I've just heard a strange incident over my telephone. It sounded as though someone was being assaulted and then I heard a gun being fired."

"Where was this was taking place?" asked the operator in a very abrupt manner.

"Well, I'm at Fairburn Sunblock on the Peninsular Trading Estate. I was in the middle of a conversation with the secretary at Salamander Advertising – they're part of Golden Salamander Film company. I don't know the actual address except to say that it's the old warehouse on Wharf Road."

"How do you know it was gun fire?"

"I can't be sure but I certainly heard them talking about a gun and someone pleading for them to put it away. It was then that I heard the bang that I thought was the gun being fired", said Lottie feeling that her common sense was in question.

"Very well, Miss Calver. I shall send police officers to investigate."

Inspector Pete Byrne in the police Operations Room was collating information from all sources and building a picture of all that happened since the attack on the airport. With the report of the emergency call from Lottie Calver, it tied in with the radio traffic from the dog handler pursuing the scent trail. The dog had actually lost the scent amongst the urban traffic near the warehouse but this call now probably pinpointed the location of the fugitives.

The telephone rang on John Churchill's desk,
"Churchill", was the terse answer.

"Hello Mr. Churchill, rather Superintendent. This is Guy Palmer at the Crenarth Post and Times. Look, I'm sorry to press you but we've sat on this story long enough. We've had the attack on the airport now and, forgive me, but it's got to be connected. This is big news and we've got all the nationals breathing down our neck. You promised me an exclusive and by the way it's going we're going to lose this."

"Yes, Guy, I'm sorry that it's broken like this. To be frank with you today's events have taken us completely by surprise. As you can understand we've been run off our feet today. Can you ring me first thing in the morning and I'll fill you in with everything that's happened so far. I guess we've no point in keeping the lid on this any longer."

Mike was beginning to feel quite weary. Most of the afternoon had been spent helping at the airport securing whatever evidence remained and organising the taking of statements from the hundreds of witnesses. It was a colossal job. The fuel tanker driver who had been the subject of the abduction gave detailed description of his four attackers which readily tied in with the four suspects.

A selection of photographs from the criminal archives was hastily produced and the photographs of the four suspects were spread amongst them to comply with the requirements of the stringent rules regarding identification of suspects by photograph. The tanker driver easily picked out the four attackers.

Teams of police officers were at the two city hospitals, trying hard to get details of all the injured and getting under the feet of the nursing staff. Tempers were getting severely stretched.

The last few hours of Mike's colleagues had been spent visiting the homes and regular haunts of the four but they seemed to have completely disappeared. Mike took the opportunity to slip home to refresh himself and perhaps get a bite to eat, knowing that he would have to return to the office to extend the search for the bombers. He quite expected to find Angie already preparing the evening meal.

As he parked in the driveway he felt a disappointment that Angie's silver mini wasn't there and the house was in darkness. He turned off the engine and the lights and struggled wearily to his feet slamming the car door behind him. He always felt it rather miserable to come home to a cold, dark house – there was always a glow about the place when Angie was there.

His key turned in the lock and he stepped inside the hall and switched on the light. He looked towards the telephone answering device but there was no flashing light. Surely she would have left a message if she intended to be late. He walked through to the kitchen and turned the dial on the wall to bring on the central heating.

Opening the refrigerator door he looked at the 'Oven Ready' dishes but wondered whether he had the time to spare to wait for Angie, 'surely she wouldn't be long'. The kettle started to sing as he unscrewed the top from the coffee jar. He couldn't help himself casting a sideways glance at the kitchen clock as he spooned the sugar into his mug.

"Half past seven. Come on Angie, this isn't like you", he said to himself, trying to suppress the anxiousness that was slowly building inside him. His thoughts focussed upon the number of hours Angie had spent waiting for him.

He carried his coffee through to the lounge and switched on the television. The program was half way through some idiotic game show and he looked for the remote – "where the hell is it? - every time I look for it, it seems to deliberately hide itself away", he said to himself; eventually finding it between the seat cushions of the settee. 'Click' , a news review; 'click' a party political broadcast to the nation; 'click' off.

He moved to the window and drew the curtains, lingering to look out at the street beyond in the hope of seeing Angie's car. Mike adjusted the curtains to hang neatly and then turned to pick up a book from the coffee table, but as he did so the pager began to bleep in the pocket of his jacket thrown on the armchair. He switched off the piercing bleeps and searched his pockets for his mobile which he quickly found, flipped it open and tapped in Alan Birchall's number.

"Yes Guv, you bleeped me?"

"Where are you Mike?"

"At home, grabbing a bite to eat. Why?"

"Get back here as quick as you can. We've got a firearms situation. I think we've got our terrorists holed up in an old warehouse".

"OK Guv. On my way", he answered replacing the mobile in his pocket.

The adrenalin rush began immediately and all thoughts of Angie being late went from his mind. Gulping down the hot coffee burnt his mouth and throat and he regretted his haste. Taking the pad of yellow 'post it' notes he wrote 'Angie, Sorry, had to go back to work. Don't know what time I'll be back. Ring you later. Mike', and he tore off the top copy and stuck it to the refrigerator.

Chapter 21

Inside the Cordon.

The journey back to the office seemed to fly by as he tried deep breathing to calm the excitement; feeling the adrenaline rush. Still totally unaware that Angie was involved, he tried to prepare his mind to be dealing with
the four terror suspects. Springing up the stairs two at a time, he was breathing heavily as he reached the Special Branch office. Alan Birchall and John Churchill were already engaged in briefing Terry Jones, Will Smith, Andrew Parr and David Scott, whilst Ron Tasker was busy arming them with their personal weapons.

"Mike, sorry to fetch you back. I'll just go over this again to bring you up to speed. This afternoon traffic section were called to a burned out car that we think was connected to the airport attack. A dog handler was called to the scene and his dog followed a scent through the country lanes to the Blackwater Estate but it was lost somewhere down near the river. Then at 6.53 this evening we received a telephone call from a lady called Lottie Calver who is employed at a firm called Fairburn Sunblock on the Peninsular Trading Estate and she reported that she was engaged in a telephone conversation with the secretary of the Golden Salamander film and advertising company on Warf Road when suddenly there was some sort of disruption.

"She was still able to hear some of what was happening in the office of the film company and heard pleas for someone to put away a gun. She then apparently heard a gun-shot. As a result of this a police response car was despatched to Warf Road. The officers tried to gain access but failed."

As Alan Birchall spoke, a sudden realisation hit Mike. 'That sounds like the film company where Angie's just got her job. Good God, that explains why she was late.' He said nothing but it sent a wave of despair through his entire body..

Alan Birchall continued,

"They have reported back to HQ that they couldn't gain entry but believe there are occupants inside the warehouse who are not responding. Other officers have been called to the scene and a cordon has now been established. A senior officer is there and he's trying to establish contact with those inside. A negotiator has been contacted and he is en- route. We need to be there as soon as possible in a firearms capacity."

The knot in Mike's stomach intensified and his head began to swim, 'Golden Salamander – that's bound to be who she's gone to work for. Hell, what's happened to her?'. The fears began to build in his mind as he prepared himself with body armour. Surely that must be why she's late home. He felt quite desperate to get to the scene.

It was only a fifteen minute high speed drive following the patrol car with its flashing blue lights and siren but every minute's delay built pressure in his mind.

Their vehicles were parked about 50 yards from the warehouse and as they sprinted to the cordon they checked their weapons and body armour.

"Report to Chief Superintendent Grey at the command vehicle", instructed the uniformed sergeant at the perimeter.

"The firearms team are here Sir", announced the constable at the door of the van.

"What's the position? Have you made contact yet?" asked Mike without the niceties in addressing rank.

The Chief Superintendent looked at Mike with some disdain; this simple discourtesy setting them off on the wrong foot. Mike's reputation had obviously preceded him.

"There's been no contact yet. They know we're here but they're choosing to keep quiet at the moment. We want them to replace the telephone receiver so that we can use the line", Grey said.

Mike had the real fear that if he said anything about Angie being held hostage, those in charge would insist he stand down. He had to be there to rescue Angie.

"O.K. I'm going forward to recce the place", said Mike.

"Very well sergeant but don't take matters into your own hands. Remember who's in charge here."

Mike looked him directly in the eyes, a look that spoke volumes, but he bit his tongue, and said nothing. As he left the command post the constable acting aide-de-camp handed Mike one of the personal radios with the dedicated channel that covered the scene.

Once in front of the warehouse his fears were all confirmed. The bright flood-lights from the police generator reflected off the silver coloured Mini Cooper parked in the loading bay. That huge knot in his stomach grew even bigger. Alongside the mini was a black BMW which immediately rang bells in Mike's memory and the pictures began to form in his mind's eye of all that he's seen on that night of his aberration. That was the car he'd seen at Goulder's home the night he'd gone there in the dark with intentions of compromising Goulder by immobilising his car.

His mind clicked into place and the Omar Sharif look-alike that Sie had captured in the photographs suddenly required no explanation; he was the driver of the BMW on that evening and was obviously connected with this film company.

Mike carefully skirted the building and approached the rear where he cast a professional eye over all the windows at ground floor level and found them secured as though they had never been opened for decades. The double doors were firmly secured and there was little chance of an escape route for the terrorists as there was a police presence at either end of the wharf and no boats were tied up.

He returned to the command post and briefed Alan Birchall. Despite his fears about being stood down, he felt he needed to tell someone.

"Listen Guv. I'm concerned about this, It looks as though my wife's in there, her mini's parked in the loading bay."

Unfortunately Chief Superintendent Grey was listening to the conversation and interjected,

"Look, if you're personally affected by this then you shouldn't be involved. All the recommendations and advice are that no-one with a personal issue should be allowed to become involved in an incident of this nature, especially involving firearms."

Mike turned away with a look of disgust,

"I'll be the bloody judge of that. If you expect me to calmly walk away from this you must be mad. It sounds to me as though you're quoting from a damn text book."

"If I consider that you are in any way compromised by your personal considerations I shall have no hesitation in forcing your withdrawal and be very careful how you speak to me", snapped Grey.

Mike walked away with a retort of "What a bloody idiot". Alan Birchall stepped in to placate Grey,

"Derek, leave it. Let me have a word with my sergeant; I'll put him straight. Can I ask you, have you ever dealt with a hostage situation like this before? No? I thought not. Would you take some advice from someone who has? I found that emotions run high in a situation like this and God only knows Mike has good reason to feel that way".

"Look here Alan, I might not have dealt with a hostage situation before but I've done enough study of regulations and Home Office recommendations and attended enough seminars on this subject to be au-fait with this. The Chief Constable must have considered me competent to deal with it or he wouldn't have appointed me and I can certainly do without some jumped up junior mouthing off at me".

"OK. I understand what you say and, yes, Mike was out of order, but he's one of my best officers and I have the utmost faith in him. All I'm trying to get across to you is that he's an exceptional officer, trained in firearms situations, who's been tried and tested and his lack of niceties is understandable in the circumstances".

"Alright, we'll agree to let the matter drop – I've more to think about than some petty insubordination, but understand this I shall keep my eye on him and if I consider that his wife's situation is affecting his judgement I shall have no hesitation in pulling him off this job. I don't want to face the prospect of an armed officer
taking unilateral action that brings the weight of the press down on all of us – or worse still, gets someone killed".

The control radio suddenly crackled into life,

"Control, receiving? A115, over"

"Go ahead 115" answered the operator.

"Hello control. I've secured an observational position on the roof of a van parked on the road. I can see into the office with my rifle scope and can see at least two women bound and gagged. There are at least two men moving about and one of them certainly has a handgun. A115 over".

"All received 115. Can you give a description of the men. Control Over".

"Hello control, yes. The one in view at the moment is the one with the handgun. It looks as though its some sort of automatic, certainly not a revolver. He's tall, about five-ten, might even be six foot. I can only see him from the waist up so it's hard to tell. I'd say he was very early twenties. He's got jet black hair and unless I'm very mistaken I'd say he was Asian. He's wearing a white shirt under a mottled brown jacket. Hold on, the second one's in view now. He's a bit older, not quite as tall and looks about twentysix or twentyeight. Black hair again. Certainly another Asian – pock marked face and a whiskery beard. He's wearing a blue jacket. I don't see any weapon. A115 over".

"Thank you 115. All received. I opened up the channel so that all officers could hear. Maintain your position and report anything fresh. Control out".

Chief Supt Grey stood at the radio operator's shoulder as he listened to the radio conversation and then turned to Alan Birchall,

"Does that fit in with what you've been telling me about these terrorists and the airport attack?"

"Yes, I'm sure it does. I'm going to send some photographs over to your observation point. We need the officer to identify the people he's observing from the photos. We've got to establish some sort of contact with them and that might pose another problem. Do they speak and understand English? We might have to bring in an interpreter".

The aide-de-camp approached Grey,

"Good news Sir, I've had GPO engineers working with us. They've instigated some sort of high pitched noise through the telephone in the warehouse office and someone has put the receiver back on its cradle. We can try to get someone to answer the 'phone now and perhaps establish contact".

"Now we're moving", said Grey wiping the sweat from his brow.

"Alan, come and share your thoughts with me. I've sent for the structural plans of the building. Now I've got to consider power and water. It's an option to turn off power and water to the building but we've got the hostages to think about. What are your views?"

"Well, as I see it, at this moment to turn off either power or water will do us little good, in fact it might be detrimental to us because without light our observation into the office will be lost. It might well be a consideration
for later. I understand your thinking, to make them disoriented and dependent upon us, but for the time being let's leave that in abeyance. Another thing to be considered is food. The longer this goes on food becomes a weapon in our armoury".

"Well, we're still waiting for our negotiator to arrive so I suppose I'd better try to get these jerks on the line and try to find out what's happening."

"OK Derek. There's just one more thing to consider – not just now, but as this progresses – that is someone to build up a psychological profile of these people. That can show up their weaknesses and it's a good tool to have when you're negotiating".

A sudden 'CRACK' rent the quiet of the evening.

"God, was that what I think it was? Get 115 on the radio, quickly, what can he see?"

"Control to A115, receiving over?"

"Yes, A115 receiving, go ahead Control, over".

"What was that 115, was it gun fire?", control over.

"I'm not sure. There's some sort of argument going on between these herberts. I don't know what's happening between them. A115 over".

"OK 115, maintain your position. Control out".

"Hello control. Wait please. I'm reporting a positive identification of one of the terrorists. He's the gun wielding man who's wearing the brown jacket. I've got the photo's in front of me now and I'm sure he's Yuseff Khan. I'm not so sure about the second man. It could be Ahmed Al-Bukhari but I've not been able to eye-ball him yet. A115 over."

"Thank you 115. All received, well done. Maintain your position. Control out."

"Sir, can someone deal with the press. They're here at the perimeter tape and they're trying to tell me they've got some special arrangement with Special Branch", said the sergeant.

"Special arrangement", said Grey turning to look at Alan Birchall.

"Ah, yes, leave it with me. I understand what they're saying. I'll go and brief them", answered Birchall.

"God, we shall have the bloody television cameras here next", said Grey.

Chapter 22

A way in.

Mike was standing well back in the shadows trying to get some perspective on the building and assessing points for a forced entry. The blue and white tape that stretched across the road was blowing in the wind and creating a vibration that he found a little irritating. He became vaguely aware of an elderly gent, wrapped up in a large shabby overcoat against the cool evening air standing on the other side of the tape. The man spoke to Mike,

"What's happening mister?"

"Don't put yourself in danger, mate. We've got some idiots inside the warehouse with guns", Mike replied.

"Guns? There's some of them Salamander people still in there", the old gent said.

"Yes we know…", answered Mike, "….How come you know who's in there?"

"I look after the place at night. I always lock up and check to make sure there's no fire risk, and so on", he answered.

"Have you got keys to the place?"

"Yes."

"What's your name?".

"Jack. Jack Lord."

"Right Jack, will you come with me? I want you to tell me all about the warehouse. I need to know how I can get in there without being seen."

"Well mister, if I was trying to get in there without being seen I'd go in through the place next door – I've got the keys for that place as well. I can take you up onto the top floor. There's an adjoining door – the only trouble is it's never been used for at least forty years so it might be difficult to get open. If you can get in there you won't be seen - but you'll need a torch there's no electricity on the top floor. I can take you up there but I'm not going in that place, I saw more than enough guns during the last war."

"OK Jack. Just hang on while I get a torch from my car and you can take me up to take a look at that door."

Jack drew a large bunch of keys from his pocket and unlocked the warehouse that adjoined the Golden Salamander Film company's building. As they went inside Jack fumbled for the light switch.

"No, don't switch the lights on, let's use my torch – I can shade that so it's not obvious to anyone outside."

"Well, just shine into my cupboard here; I shall need my own torch if I'm not going to use the lights."

"OK Jack, but try not to let your torch show to anyone watching outside."

They climbed the three flights of stairs at a rather snail pace as Jack puffed along behind Mike. The empty floor echoed to their footsteps and the dust of years was disturbed to billow up and drift in the torch beams.

"This is the door. It takes you through into a similar room in the other building. I don't think it's used –at least it wasn't the last time I was up there", said Jack.

"What's on the floor below that?"

"Well, if my memory serves me right it's full of packing cases and some small pieces of scenery. It's a while since I ventured up there. There might be some rolls of cable, but that's about all. There's a lift in one corner they use to bring the heavy stuff up onto that floor – it's just a wire cage."

"OK. Now the ground floor – describe that to me".

"It's a bit of a jumble. There's the big double doors as you know, and a smaller door set into the left hand of the doubles. They have a steel bar that lifts into place across the doorway so if that's in place you'd need a bull-dozer to break them open. There's another door to the left that the office staff use, that'll be locked too. They've spent a hell of a lot of money in there. They've had a new concrete floor laid and to the left, at the back, they've built a toilet block and changing rooms – all very modern. Then in the corner it's the office."

"It sounds as though it's a big floor space?"

"It's fairly big but most of the time there's so much clutter in there. There's rolls and rolls of cable, lighting equipment and trailers, generators, oh, and a fork lift."

"So, if I can get down there, there's plenty of cover?"

"Why, are you expecting them to use their guns?

"I shalln't know until I get in there, but from what I've been told there's already been gun fire."

"Well, yes, there's plenty of stuff to hide behind but whether or not it would stop bullets, I don't know, and anyway, you'll be totally exposed as you go down the stairs so it's a big risk."

Mike carefully examined the connecting door – it was well and truly fast, locked and probably bolted from the other side. Although it was old, it was a stout construction of thick oak tongue and groove boards that showed no sign of deterioration; truly a problem to overcome.

"Right Jack, I've seen what I wanted to see. Lets go back downstairs. Just one more question, can you leave the key to this place with me? I promise I'll get it back to you later".

"Of course" answered Jack as they picked their way back down the stairs.

Back at the command centre the vehicle was a hive of activity. A new face greeted him as he stepped inside and a friendly nod was all the introduction that was necessary, but Alan Birchall spoke up to say,

"Mike, this is Superintendent Andrews. He's our negotiator."

"Yes, John and I go back a long way...", replied Mike, "....We've worked together before", and the two shook hands warmly.

Mike turned away and poured himself a half cup of black coffee from the pot that was forever bubbling away on the hotplate. He used just one spoonful of sugar but refused the milk. He sipped gingerly at the scalding hot coffee and grimaced as the hot liquid hit his palate.

"John, I don't know whether the Governor has told you but my wife's one of the hostages in there."

"Yes, he's told me – I'm sorry....", the Superintendent answered, "...I'll do my best for you Mike."

Mike said nothing more about Angie's predicament but inside he was burning up with anxiety and asked,

"Have there been any developments?

Alan Birchall was quick to answer,

"Well since we identified Khan, the only other development is that they picked up the telephone when we rang but all that happened was that they shouted something unintelligible into the 'phone and then slammed down the receiver. We're just going to try again", and turning to John Andrews he said, "Try them again, John. Put it on speaker."

After some moments the receiver was lifted but no-one spoke.

"Come on, speak to me someone", said John showing his frustration, but still there was no answer.

"OK, if you don't want to speak to me just listen to what I've got to say. You're in a very serious position. You've no means of escaping. The whole place is surrounded by armed police, and please, be under no illusion, if you use your weapons or harm any of your hostages you will be shot. Those are the ground rules but if you're reasonable and choose to release your hostages, you'll be treated reasonably in return. Now, is anyone going to talk to me? You must have a reason for doing this. Speak to me, tell me what it is that you want."

The telephone went dead as the receiver was replaced.

"It's going to be a long night", John said aloud to no-one in particular.

Mike pulled Alan Birchall aside and spoke in low tones,

"Guv, I can get into the place next door. There's a connecting door on the top floor but I shall have to break through because we can't get the door open. Once I've broken through I can work my way down to where they're holding Angie. What do you say?"

"It's certainly an option, Mike, but it's risky isn't it. Look Mike, I know you're desperate to release Angie but we've got to look at the over view. If we go in - and we might have to in the end - there's almost certainly going to be a fire fight and we've got to be protective of the other hostages, however many there might be. So what I'm saying for now is let's try the well trodden path with negotiations. At the moment we don't know how many targets there are or how many hostages we're dealing with."

The response was no more that Mike expected but, never-the-less, he couldn't help that despondent feeling in the pit of his stomach and he itched to do something positive.

A brief rap of knuckles on the door preceded the uniform constable entering the command centre and he looked to Chief Superintendent Grey as he spoke,

"Sir, I have a Councillor Goulder here with me. He's seeking information about his wife".

"Hello Councillor, how can we help?" said Grey.

"I came down here knowing nothing about this. My wife's the owner of this company, Golden Salamander, and I was a little concerned that she hadn't returned home. What's going on? I can't get through on the telephone."

"Well, I'm sorry to tell you that we've got a bunch of armed men in there and they're holding hostages. I'm afraid your wife is likely to be one of the hostages."

"Oh my God. Why didn't someone tell me?"

"The simple truth is we don't know who's in there. We've been struggling to get information from the City council regarding planning and rates, hoping that we'd find out who owned the building".

"Well, I own the building but my wife runs the business here."

"Is there any chance that she might have records of personnel at home?"

"I don't know. The only chance is that she might have something in her computer. I'll go and check but it all depends upon whether or not I can find her password to access her files."

"Yes Sir, if you'd please try. We desperately need to know who these hostages are."

"OK I'll go back home and try. For God's sake don't let anything happen to my wife."

Chapter 23

Disharmony and bloodshed.

Javed's pain from his wounded thigh was becoming more intense and he was trying to avoid placing any weight upon the leg. The thigh muscle had set hard and burned and stung in equal measure.

"We'll just have to get you to a hospital, Javed. You need antibiotics quickly otherwise you're going to get blood poisoning", said Ahmed.

"No hospitals. No."

"But, look at you, you're sweating so you're obviously in pain. If you're not careful you'll go into shock."

"No hospitals. That means surrender".

"You've lost a lot of blood; you need medical attention", Ahmed continued.

The quiet was suddenly disturbed by another 'crack' from the office next door and the door of the washroom bust open and Yuseff rushed in. Ahmed jumped to his feet,

"What's happened?"

"I've shot that traitor. He tried to struggle free. I had no choice."

"Have you lost your mind, Yuseff? Give me the gun", demanded Javed.

"No. I must have a weapon".

"I warned you before. Don't you realise we need the hostages – they're our passport out of here. Now, give me the gun."

"No. I'm keeping it. You're injured and there's no way you can get us out of here. Look at you, you're sweating with pain and you can hardly hobble about. I shall take charge."

"Don't be stupid. You're hot headed and you're going to get us all killed. Give me the gun."

Yuseff walked away stuffing the gun into the waistband of his trousers. Ahmed looked despairingly at Javed and said,

"The idiot hasn't even put the safety catch on. He'll shoot himself next."

Yuseff and Aashif dragged Jamil's body amid the wailing of the girls from the office to the washrooms where he was left in a crumpled heap.

"Javed, what are we going to do? The police surround us; they've set up flood lights. I've had a look around and we've got no way out", said Ahmed wringing his hands.

"Have faith in Allah my brother. He will not fail us. The hostages will still provide our way out."

"They keep trying to get us on the telephone but I won't speak to them, I can't, I don't know what to say. Won't you come back in there, it's warmer and you'll be able to answer the telephone?"

Javed struggled to his feet saying,

"Help me brother", and he placed his arm over the shoulders of Ahmed who supported him to the office where he was lowered gently into a chair near the telephone.

Angie shifted uneasily in her chair, the cable ties were holding her fast and restricting her circulation. Her legs were aching from being fixed in a rather awkward position. She tried to speak and attract Javed's attention but the tape around her mouth reduced her efforts to an unintelligible murmur. Helen had virtually withdrawn inside herself. Her tear stained face had all but dried.

"Remove the tape from her mouth, let her speak", said Javed and Aashif pulled away one end of the tape leaving it dangling.

"Let us go, please. We can't do you any harm. Surely Allah doesn't wage war on women", she pleaded.

Janice and Angie exchanged pensive glances but felt helpless. Javed simply ignored her and just at that moment the telephone rang out again. All eyes were once again focused upon Javed and the telephone. He sat for some moments which, to the others, made the ringing seem more intense and urgent the longer he left it.

From the observation point on the roof of the van came the radio alert,

"A115 to control, over"

"Go ahead 115"

"I have eyeball; another ident. Javed Mustaffa Bakkar; this is a positive, repeat positive. He's sitting at the desk and just lifting the telephone receiver. I can take him out if you give the order. A115 over".

"Received 115. Good work. Maintain your position and hold your fire. Control over".

Javed raised the receiver so very tentatively to his ear and spoke in an almost placid tone into the mouthpiece,

"Allah be praised. Light upon light; He guides to his light whom He will. Allah knows everything."

"Yes, Javed, Allah knows everything and so do we", said John Andrews intending to shock Javed by using his name and he achieved his objective. It certainly took him by surprise and caused him to wonder how they were able to identify him. He looked to the window and realised that although the office was some eight feet above ground level the police must have a vantage point with a view into the office. He placed his hand over the mouthpiece and snapped orders to the others to shut the blinds.

"Javed, Tell me, just what is it that you're trying to achieve?"

"Jihad."

"Jihad? Holy war? You're obviously a devout believer so what is it that you're fighting against?"

"We fight to make the world listen. The British government are lying. They act in secret allowing their evil American allies to flout international law, imprison and torture Muslims. They support Israel in its oppression and do nothing to stop them seizing our brothers' lands."

"Well, if you're trying to make everyone listen you've certainly achieved that. Everyone will have taken notice of you after today. You've already achieved your desire so there's no need to carry it any further. Set your hostages free now and everyone will have more sympathy with you."

"Hostages stay."

"What do Yuseff Khan and the others have to say about this? Are you their leader; do you speak for them?"

"Hostages stay", repeated Javed and with that replaced the receiver.

"He's terminated the connection and what's more he's closed the blinds on the window so now we've lost our observations into the office", Andrews said in turning to Alan Birchall.

"We are going to have to resort to fibre optics. Do we have them available?"

"Yes, we do. The tactical firearms team are fully equipped."

They both turned to the coffee pot for a little inspiration as Grey deployed the team to silently drill through the window frame and insert the lense and microphone of the fibre optic camera. Andrews and Birchall sat facing each other in thoughtful silence as the door opened and in stepped Goulder. He said,

"I've manage to get the names of eight people, including my wife, who could be in there. Those names include the camera men and sound technicians. Some of them could be out on projects or simply gone home. I'd normally expect just three to be in the office, my wife Janice, the clerk Helen Cross and the new girl, Angela Borman – she's the wife of one of your officers."

"That's very helpful, Sir. Thank you", said John Andrews.

"What are you doing to get them out? What's your strategy?"

"Well, Sir, our strategy is really dictated by the fact that there are hostages in there and whilst they are not being mistreated we must tread carefully and put our faith in negotiations."

"Look here Superintendent, I'm not stupid enough to think you should go storming in risking innocent lives but you must realise that the hostages must be going through hell in there. Have you considered bringing in the SAS?" asked Goulder.

"I fully appreciate your concern, Councillor, but we're not at that position yet. To bring in the army we're accepting that there's going to be gun play, and with it the possibility, even likelihood, that a hostage will be injured or worse. We have our own men here who are trained in exactly that exercise if the need arises but that has to be a last resort..." explained

Andrews, "...Can I suggest that you have a cup of coffee and try to relax whilst we get on with our job."

A uniform constable stuck his head inside the control room and said,

"Excuse me, Sir, but you'll want to know, we've got the television cameras here. They want to speak to 'The Officer in Charge', and they're being very pushy."

"Well keep them outside the exclusion zone. Pushy or not - No exceptions. Tell them I'll be issuing a statement very soon", said Grey.

The message was relayed back to the team of camera-men and presenters at the blue and white tape as they set up their equipment in readiness. Their arc lights bathed the roadway as the male presenter addressed the camera. "Camera roll. Take one" said the producer and the presenter began to speak.

"This is Jonathan Green reporting for SC4 at Crenarth the scene of a siege at this former warehouse where gun men are holding several people hostage in the offices of a small film company. Earlier today we saw the outrage of the terrorist attack on Crenarth's airport and the belief at this moment is that the same people are involved here." The camera panned round to cover the old warehouse and then took in the police control unit and the ring of officers holding the secure area. As the producer wrote on his clip-board a by-stander walked up to him and said,

"Hello there", and offering his hand he continued, "I'm Guy Palmer of the Crenarth Post and Times. I can offer you a little back-ground to this".

"OK Mr....er....Palmer, did you say? What can you tell us?", asked the producer.

"Well, I've been involved with the police for the past week and a half. It all began with a body found in a burned out car..." and he proceeded to relate the story of his involvement.

"Right Mr. Palmer, will you do an interview to camera with our presenter, Jonathan?"

"Well, it seems I might as well because we've lost the exclusive on this", answered Palmer.

Chapter 24

A prisoner

Mike felt chilled but although the night air was quite cold, the shivers that went down his spine were undoubtedly down to his nervous tension. His personal radio sparked into life.

"Control to all officers. Control to all officers. We now have visual and audio into the office by fibre optics. We now know we're dealing with four, repeat four, terrorists. It appears that at least two of them are in possession of handguns which seem to be automatic pistols. There are three hostages, all of them women. They are all bound and gagged. This message is for information only. Control out".

"Oh God, keep Angie safe" he thought and immediately reflected on his agnostic and sceptical beliefs. He'd not been inside a church other than for his own wedding and the funeral of his parents, since his child-hood. In his mind he criticised himself for uttering such a plea to a God he had all but renounced. Then he remembered something his grandfather had told him as he had anticipated his last moments on earth; 'There were no atheists in the trenches of the Somme. Everyone chose to pray to God, believe me'.

It was certainly going to be a long night with plenty of time on his hands to worry himself about Angie and he needed to be involved, doing something constructive. He looked about for old Jack Lord but there was no sign of him. A clock somewhere chimed out the hour, and he looked to his wristwatch to check the time, 1am. He must have gone home to his bed where any sensible person would be.

He looked around him and saw that he was alone. The other officers were either maintaining their positions on the target area or guarding the exclusion zone. He felt in his pocket and produced the key Jack had left with him. He turned off the police radio and made sure that his mobile 'phone was off too.

He quietly placed the key into the lock of the warehouse door next to the target premises and let himself inside. A dull 'crack' came from the adjoining building and although muffled, Mike recognised it as gun fire. His mind was in turmoil wondering what the devil was happening next door and fearing for Angie's safety. His heart was pounding, his breathing difficult and his senses acute, as he took stock.

The darkness was almost total after leaving the street lights and police floodlights and he stood for quite some moments to accustom himself to his new environment. Shading the beam of his torch with his hand, he looked around. He hadn't noticed on his last entry into the building but the ground floor seemed to be stacked with huge bags, the shape of envelopes that were stitched up along the top edge. He poked them and found they gave easily as though packed with something very soft. He sniffed the air and realised there was the smell of sheep; huge bags of wool were stored there.

Under the broad stair case was Jack's cupboard His torch lit up the small area and he could see Jack's table that held his electric kettle and brewing commodities. The shelves were heavy with tins of paint. Under the table and in the corner away from the door was a stack of wooden boxes brim full with a jumble of bits and pieces. He emptied most of the first box which he found full of electrical switches, plugs, sockets, etc., then moved to the second box which contained paint brushes, trays and rollers. At the bottom of the pile was the box that interested him most – tools. Mike lifted the box onto the table and carefully laid out spanners, wrench, hammer, mallet, (now he felt he was getting somewhere), chisels, plane, brace and several bits.

Choosing the brace and a one inch bit he left the cupboard and climbed the stairs to the first floor. There was a dank, musty smell about the place although he still thought that the smell of the sheep wool pervaded. Up again he climbed to the top floor where, again, the dust kicked up to float lazily in the torch beam and caused Mike to sneeze. He tried to suppress it but without much success and the noise seemed to echo in the empty room. He felt a real urgency to get into the warehouse next door but knew that haste could be his downfall. Standing very still he listened carefully to convince himself that no-one had heard him. The tension was so high he could feel the blood pulsating in his ears.

Shining his torch on the connecting door he selected an area above the bottom frame and drew an area with his finger in the dust that would be large enough to crawl through. Fixing the boring bit into the brace he began in the top corner to drill the Oak board. Sticking to the outline he'd drawn in the dust he very quietly drilled hole after hole, frequently stopping to peer through into the darkness beyond and listen.

He lost track of the time he was taking but the anxiety still kept that dreadful knot in his stomach and the sweat running down his face. With the drilling of the last hole he placed the brace on the floor and placed his heel against the boards and pushed. There was a splintering, and as the panel gave way he was afraid the noise would alarm the gun men below. He sat quietly for some time, breathing deeply, trying to calm his nerves, but there was no movement or light on the other side.

He knelt before the hole and pushed head and shoulders through. It was a tight fit, tighter than he'd estimated and the edges left by the drill bit left sharp points that caught on his clothing and scratched his torso. He withdrew and removed his bulky body armour, discarding it before attempting again. This time he scraped his upper body through; his legs followed reasonable easy. Once on his feet he stood in the darkness to listen but could hear nothing other than the blood pounding in his ears.

All seemed deathly quiet and he thought of Angie; what was happening to her, was she coping with the trauma, had she been injured, did these terrifying men know that she was the wife of a police officer and if they did was that a further reason to treat her badly.

He tried very hard to push such thoughts to the back of his mind but it was almost impossible. He found himself praying to a God that he'd always believed didn't exist, making promises in his head that if Angie came through her ordeal he would do anything – just anything – as a personal penance.

He shook himself, trying desperately to concentrate his mind on what he was doing. The adrenalin was certainly pumping around his body and he knew well enough that his senses were honed to a peak if only he could detach himself from his inner worries.

Trying to picture in his mind what old Jack had told him about the place he reached out with his fingertips to feel his way along the wall to where the staircase should be. Every step was a very slow movement fearing that there might be something to stumble over, but all was as Jack had described and that floor was empty.

The stairs were a challenge in the dark and he was afraid that some deterioration might be the reason for the top floor being unused. Each step was very tentative as he tested his weight upon each tread but becoming more confident with each move.

Every footstep created a small creaking noise that to Mike's mind was enough to wake the dead. He stumbled on the last step at the foot of the first staircase and he fell. The noise of his fall seemed to echo and he lay where he fell, waiting for what he believed was inevitable discovery. A door opened and bright light flooded the ground floor. He held his breath and reached under his jacket to his holstered Walther PPK and gently slid the weapon clear in readiness.

The tingling of his nerves and the effort to control the noise of his breathing were almost exhausting. He wiped the beads of sweat from his brow then remained motionless, listening intently for those tell tale footsteps on the stairs - but none came. Instead, he heard the sound of the door being closed again and once again the ground floor was in darkness.

The shrill tones of a telephone ringing somewhere below broke the stillness and there were murmurs of male voices before the ringing stopped. Just one male voice could be heard, probably speaking to the telephone, but he couldn't make out what was being said. It was an opportunity to cross the floor to the next stairs whilst the attention of those below was taken by the telephone call. From the head of the next staircase he could see a faint light under a door to the right on the ground floor and further forward was a slightly stronger light from a small window in another door.

After being in the dark for such a long time this small amount of light was a welcome relief. The sound of raised voices was coming from behind the door where the light was escaping from that small window.

Mike took the opportunity to make a final dash to the ground floor so that he wasn't exposed for so long but first he checked that the ammunition clip of his Walther PPK was seated properly – now wasn't the time for a mis-fire. He pulled back the slide to project a round into the chamber and slipped the safety catch off. With his torch in his left hand, ready for use, he quickly and quietly descended the stairs to the concrete of the ground floor.

His heart pounding like some massive steam hammer, he slid behind two packing cases and waited again. This really was a fools game that in rational times, even in training, he would never contemplate. He was going into the lions den – without body armour.

He stood to one side of the door that was showing a light beneath it and he listened hard but could hear nothing beyond the door. He pushed it very slightly ajar and peered inside. It had the appearance of a tiled toilet block. His heart missed a beat as he saw the bloodstains that indicated something had been dragged along the floor tiles. He stepped inside and looked around and his eyes fell on some pieces of cloth on the floor near the hand basin. He picked up a cloth and his fears were immediately confirmed – it was blood and fresh.

His worst nightmare – was it Angie's blood, had she been injured? Heart in mouth, he pushed open an inner door to some sort of changing room and almost fell over the body crumpled on the floor.

Mike's feelings were so mixed up there was almost relief when he saw the body was that of a middle aged man. Taking hold of the dead man's shoulder he turned the body so that it was lying on it's back. It was almost second nature to check for a pulse at the carotid artery, but in vain. That familiar face was staring glassy eyed at him and he recognised the Omar Sharif image that he'd seen before.

He retraced his steps very carefully out onto the bare concrete of the warehouse floor. The door to the office was closed and Mike considered that the hostages and gunmen must be in there. His reasoning told him they must be confident that their fortress was secure. He found a hiding place behind the packing cases and tried to gather his senses. Feeling almost sick inside he gingerly made his way, behind the fork lift, to the double doors.

In the very dim light he could see the bar securing the doors that Jack had described. It was heavy but he lifted it from its brackets and quietly laid it on the concrete. The small personnel door within the large double doors was now only held by a yale lock which he fastened in the open position. Quite suddenly a shaft of light pierced the darkness as the office door began to open. He jumped back into the shadows behind the fork-lift and pressed himself flat against the vehicle, holding his breath as best he could. The silhouette of the man was clearly visible until he closed the office door behind him he then became just a shadowy blur as he made his way towards the door.

The shadowy figure seemed to stumble against something on the floor and bent down to investigate what it was. Mike's heart was in his mouth as he realised the object was in fact the bar that he'd removed from the doors.

He realised that this figure was going to discover that someone else was in the building and he'd raise the alarm. It took just seconds to over-power the man. With the stealth of a predatory cat he crept up behind the figure. His left hand went around his face and smothered his mouth whilst the right hand pressed the muzzle of his weapon hard against his temple.

The man struggled as the panic grabbed him, trying to rip Mike's hand away from his mouth. Mike's weapon was brought down with real force on the man's skull and his knees buckled beneath him.

They fell in a heap but Mike was quick to recover wary that his adversary may well be feigning unconsciousness, but there was no acting – he was out cold. He felt the warm stickiness of blood trickling from the scalp wound of the terrorist.

Mike was concerned that the others may have heard something and he waited briefly with his gun trained on the office door but there was no movement. Assured that he wasn't immediately threatened by any other terrorist appearing, he dragged the unconscious man to the door and tentatively opened it then gave several very brief flashes of his torch to alert the watching team of police outside. He didn't fancy getting shot by his own colleagues. Two of the firearms team immediately confronted Mike.

"Christ Mike, we thought it was one of the terrorist bastards."

"Ssssh...Don't raise your voice. Help me carry this prisoner out of here. He's out cold."
They hurriedly carried the unconscious man outside closing the door quietly behind them.

At the control van Mike opened the door and caught Alan Birchall's eye and beckoned him outside, away from Grey and others ears.

"I've brought you a prisoner Guv. He's only just coming round – I'm afraid I had to hit him over the head."

"How the hell have you managed this?"

"I've been inside, Guv, and I've made it easy for the entry-team to get in."

"Bloody hell, Mike. You do take matters into your own hands. Grey'll go ballistic. It's his show Mike and he's already set the stage for a waiting game."

"Yes, I know Guv, but it's not his bloody wife who's being held in there and the game has changed now. We've all heard the shots that have been fired and there's a dead hostage lying in there."

"Good God. Are you sure."

"Look Guv, I've seen him – he's dead, believe me."
"That changes things. Let's go back inside and I'll put it to Derek Grey. God only knows what he'll say. You'd better prepare yourself for trouble."

"Come on, Guv. Believe me, he's the least of my worries."
Birchall turned to go inside again then over his shoulder he said to the other two officers,

"Make sure the prisoner is restrained – and get him some first aid treatment. We shall need to question him in a moment".

Chapter 25

The End Game.

"Derek; John; can I have your attention. We've got a change in the circumstances in there with the hostages. We know that one hostage is dead. We've got first hand confirmation and we've managed to secure one of the terrorist as a prisoner", said Birchall.

"How in creation have you managed that? We've got the fibre optics and microphone into there and we've neither seen or heard anything", said Grey.

"Believe me, Mike here has been inside and he's seen the dead hostage. Not only
that but he's managed to prepare access for the assault team."

Grey put his head in his hands in despair.

"What the hell do you think you were doing Borman. You went against a direct order, knowing full well that you were putting the lives of hostages at risk".

"Oh go and soak your head you idiot. You're just upset because your little game of political correct tactics has been blown."
The colour built in Grey's face as he blustered in the face of this audacious insubordination.

"Mark my words Borman. You'll come to regret your attitude. When this is over I intend to make a full report to the Chief Constable and have you disciplined."

"Oh, just do what you want. My wife's a hostage in there and I've got to get her out."

"Where do we go from here?" said a despondent Grey to Alan Birchall.

"Well, to my mind we've no option. We've got to go in and take them out", said Birchall.

"God only knows what Goulder is going to make of all this...", then shaking his head, Grey continued, "...Right, it's decision time. If you're convinced that we should go in then that's what we shall do. I shall just have to clear it with the

ACC. Whilst I'm on to the ACC, Alan, I need you to begin to work out some form of strategy."

"Oh dear, Mike, watch your back, he's got it in for you…", Birchall whispered to Mike, then said aloud, "…Right, let's have you all around this table. Mike, the first thing is for you to draw me a decent sized map of the ground floor of the building – get to it. Whilst you're doing that Ron must consider how many men he needs for the incursion and what aids we shall need. Whilst you're doing that I'm going to see what I can get from the prisoner."

The prisoner, head swathed in bandage, was seated, handcuffed, in an ambulance with his two police guards.

"Has he been searched?" asked Birchall.

"Yes Sir. He's clean. There's just this card in his pocket – looks like something to do with his benefits – with the name Aashif Ibn-Ali Qarmati."

"Have you spoken to him?"

"Yes Sir. He speaks good English. I've read him the caution and he fully understands."

Birchall climbed inside the ambulance and sat opposite the prisoner,

"Aashif, is that your name?"

"Yes. I am Aashif Ibn-Ali, but please, Sir, my head is hurting."

"Yes, I'm not surprised Aashif, but what more did you expect? You've caused terrible injuries and destruction at the airport and now you've taken hostages and actually murdered one of them."

"No Sir, Not me Sir. I have no gun, I'm afraid to use one. The others had guns and they frightened me. I tried to stop Yuseff he was crazy, striking the man – he couldn't defend himself he was tied to a chair. When he struggled to break free and escape Yuseff shot him.

"The women were afraid and screaming and I wanted to get away. I waited until the others were trying to sleep and then I crept towards the door but somebody jumped on me in the darkness. He was choking me, I couldn't breathe and I was struggling to get air when he struck me on the head. I must have passed out."

"Your friend Javed is that Javed Mustaffa Bakkar?"

"Yes Sir."

"And Yuseff, who's he?

"Yusefff Khan. It was him who shot the man. He's gone crazy since he got the gun.Javed tried to take it off him."

"Well, who's the other?"

"Ahmed. Ahmed Al-Bukhari. He's a good man. He doesn't use a gun either."

"O.K. So only Javed and Yuseff have guns – is that correct?"

"Yes Sir. Javed is injured, here (pointing to his own leg) in the thigh. He was wounded at the airport."

"One last question Aashif, then you can go to the hospital. Have your friends any other weapons?"

"No Sir. None."

"What about explosives?"

"No Sir. Javed used all we had at the airport."

"O.K. Aashif, you'll be taken to the hospital first and then I'll see you later at the Police Station where you'll be detained."

Alan Birchall made his way back to the Control and instructed the radio operator,

"Get me Ron Tasker in here immediately".

After only a few minutes Mike produced his ground-floor plan and spread it before them.

"This is our access point...", he said pointing to the personnel door within the double doors, "...The shaded area is just a jumble of packing cases, rolls of cable, generators, lights and stands, and at the back - pieces of scenery. This here's a fork-lift truck. Over here's a staircase leading to the first floor and here's a toilet block, washing facilities and changing rooms. That's where the dead hostage is. This is the office where our targets and the hostages are. There are five steps up to the office door. It's only a flimsy door with a small panel of opaque glass."

Birchall replied,

"OK Mike, that's good. Now let me fill in what we can see of the office space from the fibre optic camera. This is the telephone corner where our man Javed Bakkar is resting – remember he's the one that's wounded.. Next to him is another of the targets that we think is Ahmed Al-Bukhari – we're not positive. Lying on the floor here directly opposite the door is Yuseff Khan. The three of them have to be considered dangerous but watch this man, Khan, in particular his profile shows him as a hot head. We know they're armed with automatic pistols but the prisoner says that only Javed Bakkar and Yuseff Khan are armed. We can't rely on that so be very careful. There are three female hostages who are bound and gagged, seated along this wall off to the right. Behind the door are three filing cabinets which unfortunately are obscuring where there could be a fourth hostage. They all seem to be in a good physical shape."

Ron Tasker was leaning over the table considering the plan and the information that was being given. Birchall said,

"Ron, I want you to take charge of this operation inside the building. We need to get in there within the next thirty minutes to take advantage of what the psychologists tell us is the human mind's lowest ebb – between two and three a.m. My suggestion, Ron, is that you choose how-ever many men you need, then formulate your own plan of action. My personal preference would be to use stun grenades into the office before making entry. Over to you Ron."

"Right, thank you Sir. I need five others and I think Sergeant Borman, David Scott and Andrew Parr have proved their worth already. I'll take Bill Parker and Clive Smithson as the other two. Mike informs me that we can get into the warehouse easily as he's removed the securing bar from behind the double doors so our access point is the personnel door within the left hand of the double doors. With a little luck we shouldn't find any opposition in the first instance, they all seem to be in the office."

Ron looked across to Clive Smithson and said,

"It strikes me that we need a point man to go to this corner that I'll mark 'A'. Clive, you can take that position and your object is to make sure that no-one emerges from this toilet block. You'll also have a view of the staircase. I'm going in first. When I get to the office I shall put two stun grenades in. It's

2.15 and if the psychologist is right, they'll be at their lowest mental edge – so here's wishing us luck.

"You all know the drill – in there fast and take the targets out. Expect smoke and a hell of a confusion so keep focussed.. Take no chances; I want no casualties amongst us. I want to stress, if there's no resistance then they'll be immobilised and restrained but, again, take no chances.

"There'll be a team of arrest officers following us in once we've secured the area. They'll release the hostages and deal with any prisoners. Now, I'll repeat, I'm going in first and my target will be Javed Bakkar, I want Mike to follow me and his target will be the man we believe to be Ahmed Al-Bukhari, David will target Yuseff Khan – and I'll stress again he's the most dangerous one. Bill will stay at the door, point 'B', that is unless he sees that one of the team needs assistance.

"Remember, we've got the element of surprise but it's going to be tight in there; we're all going in through that one doorway and so it's up to each one of us to get ourselves out of the way as quick as possible so we don't obstruct the line of sight or fire of those who are following us. Are there any questions?"

John Andrews had been listening intently to Ron's brief and he said quite innocently,

"Have you considered tasers? I know we've got them now. Are they not a possibility?"

Ron turned to look at him scornfully,

"Have you ever used a taser?"

"No, I know nothing about them. I just threw it in the mix for what it was worth."

"Well, yes, we've got tasers but they're not an option here. They're OK for a one on one situation but no use here. Has anyone else any questions before we go?"

"Don't laugh but are there any rats in there?" asked Bill, "I don't like rats."

Mike smiled as he answered,

"No, Bill. There are no rats."

"Listen up everybody…", said Derek Grey, "…We've got the ACC's go ahead. He'd like to see this resolved without gun-play but you have his support regardless. Now, I want to see you all wearing your body armour and don't forget, be careful!."

The team left the control van and gathered in the light rain under a roadside tree. Ron Tasker instructed,

"OK, check your gear. Make sure your Maglights work and ammo clips are properly seated, check the slide and feed – malfunctions could mean disaster. Remember there's going to be a lot of smoke in there when I throw the grenade. Does everyone understand what they're supposed to do?" and he looked around the team giving time for someone to respond but everyone appeared confident in their role.

"Remember what you've been taught, hesitation is fatal so, safety first. There's no such thing as shooting to wound – body mass and double tap every time. Lets go."

The team went in single file taking advantage of what meagre cover was available.

"Radios off", Ron hissed, and waited for acknowledgement from each one. At a sprint they climbed onto the loading bay then hesitated as Ron gently pushed at the personnel door. It swung open with only the slightest of noise. He waited and listened but there was no movement or sound. Mike felt the adrenalin surge through his blood-stream. His whole body felt like a coiled spring and his temples pounded like the taught skin of a drum. He stretched his fingers before tightening his grip on his Walther PPK. He knew Angie and the other girls were going to go through hell as the office erupted into bedlam and terror, but this was no time for a wandering mind, he had to be focussed.

Their entry into the warehouse was quiet but fast and furious – tactics they had rehearsed time and again in training scenarios. Each one took their designated position. Their rubber soled footwear made only the slightest sound upon the concrete and Ron crept cautiously onto the five steps leading to the office. He looked behind him in the dim light to check that the team were ready and removed the two stun grenades from his belt. He held them aloft so that Mike, his number two could see them, and then pulled the primers. Shock tactics – counting to five, he grasped the door handle and in one swift movement pushed the door ajar and lobbed the grenades inside.

Immediately there was a terrific 'bang' that echoed through the building and in that split second Ron forced the door wide open and ran inside. His maglite in his left hand alongside the Browning in his right. The pencil beam cut through the smoke and he scanned the room as he ran. The loud, hyper-excited shouting of "Armed Police" from the team as they made their entry was as much an assault on the minds and senses of the terrorists as the weapons they faced. Other maglights beamed behind him and the room became awash with a kaleidoscope of light. The thin smoke caught in his throat. His target, Javed, was struggling to his feet from the chair in a completely disoriented state.

Ron's index finger tightened slightly until he felt the pressure of the trigger in an excited readiness to fire his weapon, but he held his nerve and pulled Javed backwards to fall to the floor. The terrorist's weapon fell to the floor and Ron kicked it far into the corner where it couldn't be reached. In one quick movement he rolled Javed onto his stomach and forced the barrel of his automatic into the back of his neck.

'Crack, crack' came the report of Mike's gun behind him, which made him momentarily turn seeing the figure of a man fall from a kneeling position to lie crumpled on the floor, moaning.

Mike had followed Ron closely and had made for his target Ahmed but as he crossed the room he caught sight of Yuseff rising to a kneeling position with his weapon being raised to a firing position. He was going to fire at Ron's unprotected back. It was an auto-reflex action to fire taking Yuseff down, and as he fell Mike landed a vicious kick into his victim's ribs. Ensuring Yuseff couldn't pose a threat any longer, he stood on the wounded terrorist's wrist whilst he ripped the automatic from his grasp.

Ron looked at Mike but no words were exchanged, but in that split second there was a feeling of gratitude that passed between them.

Before the smoke had chance to clear the arrest team followed into the room. Theirs was the task to secure the prisoners with the plastic 'cuffs.

Despite Yuseff's perilous, life threatening state, he was afforded no exception. With the prisoners secured their attention was turned to the hostages and their bindings removed. Each was bundled unceremoniously out of the building to safety.

Free of his immediate responsibility Mike pushed his way outside to find Angie standing by the two ambulances that were drawn up at the roadside in readiness. They were being guarded by uniform officers. Angie was hugging Janice and Helen and all were sobbing in relief. He took Angie by the arm and pulled her gently from the communal hug. She turned to him and flung her arms around him and sobbed into his chest.

Still full of the adrenaline, he hugged her tightly and broke into tears himself. Their sobs racked their bodies as they clung to each other. Mike broke away briefly to look towards the stretcher bearing Yuseff being loaded into an ambulance.t Javed was being dragged towards the same ambulance by a uniformed officer who didn't appear to hold any sympathy. Flash bulbs from cameras seemed to come from every angle.

The clear up operation was in full swing. The freed hostages were ferried to hospital despite their objections and again Mike and Angie were briefly parted. The de-brief took place immediately within the control van.
Ron Tasker watched for Mike entering the vehicle and extended his hand and Mike shook it firmly. The gratitude was heart-felt as he said,

"Thank's mate. He'd have dropped me that's for sure."

"That's OK. That's what we trained for, isn't it?"

"Great job. Well done…", said Birchall. "…Mike, give me your gun, it's got to be submitted for forensics."

"Why, Guv?…" asked Mike, "….We all know it was me that shot the bastard."

"It's all red tape. We shall all be subject to a police complaints investigation and your gun forms part of the evidence."

"Good grief, have we got to justify ourselves now. They were bloody terrorists holding hostages for God's sake."

"Don't worry about it Mike. It's red tape that has to be followed but I personally will assure you that no blame will be attached to any of you. Now, you get off to the hospital to find Angie."

Mike stepped outside the control van into the glare of the television floodlights and cameras. The presenter pushed forward shoving a microphone into Mike's face.

"Can you tell us what happened in there? Who shot the terrorist?"

"Don't know mate, I'm just a technician", he lied as he pushed past. He walked purposefully towards his car when he perceived someone running up behind him.

"Mike, Mike. Hang on a minute", came the familiar voice and he turned to see Guy Palmer, the reporter. He hesitated as Palmer caught up with him. Breathlessly he said,

"Mike, you promised me an exclusive. What about it?"

"OK Guy, you've got it, but not now. My wife's been involved in this and I've got to get to hospital to see her."

"Is she injured?"

"Not physically. She's gone with the others for a check-up that's all...", Mike replied, "....Look, it's been a long night. Meet me at Headquarters at about two o'clock and you can have the whole story."

Guy Palmer clapped Mike enthusiastically on the back and said, "Thank's Mike, well done – go to it", and he turned away as Mike climbed into his car.

The casualty staff were approaching the end of their night shift but the excitement amongst them, learning of the incident, injected fresh life into an otherwise dull night. Yuseff was rushed to theatre; the alert having prepared both theatre and staff. There was little optimism for his chances. Meanwhile, Javed, under guard was being treated, his wound cleaned and dressed and the necessary antibiotics administered.

Elsewhere in casualty Angie, Janice, and Helen were being examined. There was concern for them all, having been trussed and unable to move their limbs for some six or more hours, that a deep vein thrombosis may result. Asprin to thin the blood and a strong sedative were prescribed to be taken when they each reached home. The order was bed rest for the next twenty-four hours.

Mike met Angie in the waiting room and she jumped to her feet and fell into his arms. She was still shivering nervously as Mike caressed her.

"Come on, let's get you home. A damned good cup of sweet tea is what we both want."

"Yes, it's going to be difficult to get to sleep."

"That's what they've given you the tablets for."

As they prepared to leave Alan Birchall appeared from the depths of the hospital together with a white coated female who carried a stethoscope around her neck. Seeing Mike and Angie he made straight for them and as he approached he asked,

"Angie, are you OK. Have they checked you over?"

"Yes, I'm OK, just very thankful to be here. They've given me tablets but what I need most is sleep."

He gave her a friendly hug and then said,

"I just need to have a quiet word with Mike, will you excuse us just for a minute?" and taking Mike by the shoulder gently led him aside.

"Just to let you know, Mike, he's dead. Died in theatre. That means an inquest".

Mike just nodded his head.

"Get off home. Get some sleep. By the way, I'm putting you in for an award, the Queen's Police Medal.

They can't keep denying it to you and this time I know we've got the Chief's support. The only fly in the ointment is Derek Grey, I shall have to talk sweetly to him."

"Thanks Guv. I know I'm an awkward bastard and not the easiest to get along with but surely these were exceptional circumstances."

"Well, come what may the Chief has virtually promised you promotion already. He has asked me to personally convey to you his thanks for a job well done."

---ooOoo---

About the Author.

The author was for some time a Special Branch Detective in the Derbyshire Constabulary. He spent time in Harrogate, Wakefield, Liverpool and London, and worked with MI5 and MI6 and very briefly the American Secret Service.

His work included personal protection for most of our Royal Family, various politicians, foreign Heads of State and also for Sir Maurice Oldfield, Ex Director General of MI6 and later Supremo for Northern Ireland during its recent turbulent times.

He was a trained firearms specialist and took part in several dangerous incidents that earned commendations from a Judge of Assize and Chief Constables.

Acknowledgements

Acknowledgement to Professor Malcolm Clark and his book Islam for Dummies (Wiley Publishing, Inc.) from which I have been able to glean the background information, historical facts, and interpretations of Islam and the Qu'ran.

Thanks also go to my wife, Margaret, who has been both my editor and agent, and who spends many lonely hours whilst I am writing.

Printed in Great Britain
by Amazon